Jet Set

Also by Carrie Karasyov & Jill Kargman

BITTERSWEET SIXTEEN
SUMMER INTERN

Jet Set

CARRIE KARASYOV
& JILL KARGMAN

HARPER TEEN
An Imprint of HarperCollins*Publishers*

HarperTeen is an imprint of HarperCollins Publishers.

Jet Set

Library of Congress Cataloging-in-Publication Data
Karasyov, Carrie.
    Jet set / Carrie Karasyov & Jill Kargman. — 1st ed.
        p.   cm.
    Summary: Lucy Peterson, the daughter of a career army man, has always been devoted
to academics and tennis, but when her tennis ability wins her a scholarship to an elite
Swiss boarding school, distractions abound and her hardest task is telling friend from foe.
    ISBN 978-0-06-143177-7 (trade bdg.)
    [1. Interpersonal relations—Fiction. 2. Wealth—Fiction. 3. Boarding schools—
Fiction. 4. Schools—Fiction. 5. Tennis—Fiction. 6. Social classes—Fiction.
7. Switzerland—Fiction.] I. Kargman, Jill. II. Title.
PZ7.K12995Jet 2008   2008000735
[Fic]—dc22   CIP
                                                                                          AC

Typography by Joel Tippie
1 2 3 4 5 6 7 8 9 10

First Edition

Acknowledgments

Jill and Carrie thank . . . the amazing HC crew: Tara Weikum, Erica Sussman, and Melissa Dittmar—you guys are the best; and the über-consigliere, Steven Beer of Greenberg Traurig.

Carrie thanks . . . all of her friends and family, agents, babysitters, and life coaches.

Jill thanks . . . the cousin posse who keep me young: Charlotte Coch, Emily Coch, Alexa Kopelman, and Julia Kopelman; the Swiss boarding school deep throat: Leigh Ofer, plus goddess Laura Tanny; Agents extraordinaire: Jennifer Joel, Elliot Webb, and Josie Freedman of ICM; the pals who lived through the rocky high school years with me: Dana Wallach, Lisa Turvey, Trip Cullman, and Lauren Duff. Plus, the chères who always support and have now known me half my life (!): Vanessa Eastman and Jeannie Stern. To the fam: Kargs & Kopes, I love you so—special mercis to Mom, Dad, Will, and Harry, plus the mini-cubs: Sadie, Ivy, and Fletcher.

Jet Set

Chapter One

*I*magine a school with endless gilded hallways that rival Versailles. A chandelier-filled dining room with a painted ceiling that echoes the Sistine Chapel. Thirty-foot-high arches as you walk into the mahogany library. Priceless collections of rare books and illuminated manuscripts. Art worthy of the Louvre. Marble from the rarest quarries. Picture a majestic castle nestled into a lush green mountainside next to a glistening river, and inside it students hailing from around the globe.

It ain't Hogwarts, people. It's my new school: the elite Van Pelt

Academy in Switzerland. And while there aren't wizards, wands, or dragons, there is plenty of magic—the storied history of generations of royal alumni, a network of global power hatched from friendships struck at age fifteen, and an air of mystery that shrouds this private school that is, without a doubt, the Who's Who of the world.

My classmates are a kaleidoscope of the world's aristocracy. The son of a Russian coal tycoon, the daughter of the deposed king of Italy, an Indian princess, a Texas oil billionaire's son, the son of an Arab emir, a jewelry house heir, a fashion empire scion, and so on. I don't know how to say the phrase "over the top" in Latin, but if I could, I would have nominated that to be the school's motto. Families had decorators flown in during the summer to design their children's rooms before September's arrival day, which was today, my first day of tenth grade. There were personal porters with piles of Vuitton steamer trunks, safes on dollies, and standing garment racks (lest the couture frocks get wrinkled accordion style in a suitcase).

Do I sound bitter? I wasn't, hand to God, I swear—I knew I was truly blessed beyond measure to be here. I just felt a tad pauperish given the illustrious backgrounds of my fellow students. Take the school store, for instance. Yours may have pens, paper, letter sweaters, the like. We had a huge glass-domed room like a London gallery, filled with booth after booth of satellite stores— a mini Chanel, Versace, Vuitton, Tiffany (and others I had never heard of)—all with bursar billing so some dynastic darling could scribble her signature, charge a fur vest to Daddy, and be off to enjoy her new purchases. So, as you can tell, it's not your normal institution. I mean, New England prep schools may be fancy, but they don't have 300-count sheets or maid service. Or room service. Or dry-cleaning service. If you went to some ivy-covered Massachusetts institution and you happened to get hungry late at night? It's called a vending machine, people. Van Pelt has a leather-bound hotel-style menu in every dorm room, listing every food you could ever dream up. Too bad there wasn't much I could afford on it. . . . I was offered a small monthly stipend with my full scholarship, but it wasn't enough to keep me afloat in this Monopoly land. People don't even bother to lock their doors here because they're all so rich, why would they need to steal anything? Safes are provided for all the royal jewels, of course.

Let me clarify how I fit into this picture. My dad is a lifelong military man, which means my family has constantly moved from place to place. But I have always been the Good Girl who did what she was told and adapted seamlessly. Being the dreaded "new girl" at school wasn't actually that bad for me; I generally thrived in academic environments, and I always had the structure of a team sport with my tennis playing. Killing on the tennis courts has been a huge feather in my Nike visor.

I had just started ninth grade when I knew I couldn't move again. I desperately wanted roots. I had been playing scholastic hopscotch too long, and my parents had promised me that I could go away to boarding school . . . if I could get myself a scholarship.

I browsed catalogs for schools in the United States dotting the Eastern Seaboard from Connecticut to New Hampshire. But something about being so far away from my family kept me from filing my applications and writing my essays, which wasn't like me. I'd never been much of a procrastinator and had gotten straight As, geek style, pretty much since they started giving grades, albeit in check-minus/check/check-plus form. I knew this would be a huge decision, and I was agonizing over where to apply when I was walking down the street in my most recent hometown (Munich) and bumped into the older sister of a friend from my school in Spain. She had just graduated from Van Pelt and raved about it with stars in her eyes, saying wistfully those years had been the best years of her life.

Hmm . . . a boarding school where I could stay for three straight years and be on the same continent as my family? I knew of a few in England but they were all single sex and supposedly all legacies. Intrigued, I logged on to the website to register my request for an application. I was emailed back a password for the private pages of the website so I could surf the myriad images of Prince William look-alikes dressed formally for class and brandishing stacks of old books, even switching to the famed Gstaad campus for the winter term, where instruction is in the morning so students can ski in the afternoon. For real. How many schools in the world switch campuses midyear to accommodate choice slalom time? One. Mine. Yeah . . . crazy.

But what really attracted me was the image of row after row of tennis courts. They had cement courts, they had clay courts, but most important of all: grass courts. The rarely seen nature's courts were the definition of high maintenance, with thrice daily mowings that made a golf course look overgrown. In all my life I had never played on grass. It had been a dream of mine, and I couldn't imagine going to a school where they would be readily available to me. I was sold. My parents were sold, my dad especially, who was determined that I get a top education and go to a top school. He thought Van Pelt was a great idea. I just needed to sell the school.

After slaving over my not one, not two, but three essay questions and fine-tooth combing my lists of extracurricular interests and aspirations, plus culling recommendations, school transcripts, and standardized test scores, I sent in the almighty application packet, which rivaled the phone book in thickness. I applied for financial aid and corresponded with the tennis coach who came to watch me in a tournament. Luckily I played the match of my life and—presto!—weeks later I received a hand-delivered acceptance letter on a calligraphy-written scroll! Maybe the other applicants hailed from schools where that kind of grandiose gesture was par for the course, but all I'd known were metal lockers and fluorescent-lit hallways—not manicured lawns and parchment mailings. I was euphoric and convinced that my years of adapting chameleonlike to school after school would help me fit in, even though I had so little in common with my glittering classmates— or at least the alums who graced the Van Pelt site.

It was only when I arrived that the nervous pit in my stomach did a flip. You know, the whole "be careful what you wish for" idea? I had wanted so badly to stay in one place for the next three years and not jump around, but now I couldn't imagine what I was thinking. I was throwing myself into the highest echelons of society that only about .5 percent of the world enjoy. In theory, I could see myself pictured in the brochure for the school—studying with them, playing tennis with them, on the lunch line with them. But in practice, would I really be able to socialize with them? They had rules that I had no idea about. How could I have thought it would be just like transferring to a school on another army base?

Okay, okay, it was only my first day. I had to remember to stay positive. And to breathe.

Chapter Two

"These are the West Stables, where you can board up to three of your horses. Additional horses have to be kept at the East Stables, which is such a drag! But you'll be happy to know that they have finally made the complete transformation to *organic* horse feed, so now we don't have to worry about our babies anymore!"

"Um, I actually don't have any babies," I said.

"Don't have any babies! You poor sweetie!" I couldn't tell if the crisp English accent was sarcastic or not.

I was being guided around campus by Sofia Glenn, a member of the Golden Key Club (a group responsible for showing new students the ropes) who had been assigned to give my tour. (I was to refer to her as my "Sister Advisor," and she was to refer to me as her "Apprentice.") She was a confident, striking blonde whose chic British tone and modelesque bod immediately made her seem older, though she was a sophomore like me. The difference was she had freshman year at Van Pelt under her belt, which made her an expert compared to my newbie self. I followed Sofia obediently around the school, passing girls clad in full riding garb, right down to suede britches and chocolate brown velvet caps that, it appeared, they wore whether or not they were on a horse. Sofia had filled me in on some general campus information on the ride to the school, and continued her dialogue on our tour. She was nice, but I could tell I was probably tour number three or four of the day and it was a bit by rote.

"Yes, I guess it's a bummer. I would love to learn how to ride, but I bet I'm hopeless," I confessed, pulling my light brown hair into a messy ponytail. Every kid I saw looked so polished. Note to self: look a tad less rolled-out-of-bed-ish.

"But I hear that you are a crackerjack on the tennis court," said Sofia.

I reddened. "Really? Who told you that?" I asked quickly.

"Word travels fast," she said, shrugging, and started down a winding path. "Everyone here is *someone*. You're the tennis star."

Huh? It's not like I was walking around in all whites toting my racket.

"I mean, I guess I'm a good player . . . "

"You must be," said Sofia with confidence. "No one here is mediocre. Everyone either has an extreme talent or . . . " She trailed off and looked away at the rolling verdant hills.

"Or?"

"Extreme wealth," she said, staring at me evenly.

"Right."

I still couldn't decide how open to be about my situation. Should I pretend to be like them or be self-deprecating and admit I was just a meager scholarship student? I didn't want to lie, and I didn't think everyone deserved the right to know my financial background, so my plan was just to try and fit in as much as I could without hiding or volunteering any information.

"Nice eyes," Sofia said, looking so intently into my pupils it was as if she could see my brain, X-ray style. I thanked her sheepishly, noticing that her eyes were even bluer than mine. I couldn't quite get a read on her.

As we exited the stables, Sofia explained the way Van Pelt worked. "The school has about five hundred students, but each grade is divided into 'sectionals'—basically classes. You'll be seeing a lot of the people in your sectional. You'll be assigned to the same tables at our dinner events, you'll have group meetings with them, and you'll have away trips with them. Basically you'll get really sick of them," she said.

I nodded. Great. I could only hope I got cool people in my "sectional."

We continued on through our tour, skipping only the ten-foot hedge labyrinth and the boys' dormitory wing (called Le Chambord). Finally it was the moment I'd been waiting for. I'd seen the pictures, but even in person I was astounded by the tennis facility. They had enough courts to host every single grand slam. I couldn't wait to get out there. I could tell that Sofia was eager to continue, but I made her linger a little more in the tennis center, where they had state-of-the-art equipment like aerodynamic ball throwers and computers that analyzed your every stroke. After a quick peek into the plush "locker rooms," replete with massage tables and massage therapists *standing by* (with buffet or your choice of aromatherapy oils), we ended up back on the floor of my dorm. I was eager to plop on my bed and digest everything, but Sofia continued to lead me down the grand arch-ceilinged hallways.

"Let me show you the lounge," she insisted. "Wait till you see this."

The "lounge" was more like a viewing room with plush chairs, plasma televisions, and a bartender waiting to take orders. There were three pretty girls comfortably ensconced on the sofas, chatting furiously in French.

"Hey, ladies," said Sofia, motioning for me to come inside. "This is Lucy Peterson, our new classmate. Lucy, this is Antigone, Iman, and Victoria."

"Hello," acknowledged Antigone curtly.

"Nice to meet you," I murmured. These were my classmates? They looked so much older! Yikes. Antigone had sleek jet black hair down to her ass and heavily lined eyes, and she was clad in so many designer logos it made my head spin. Iman was gorgeous, with skin the most wonderful latte brown and giant hazel eyes. Victoria had dirty-blond hair and what appeared to be a perpetual scowl. I noticed her give me the once-over and then glance away.

"You're the tennis player?" asked Victoria with an edge in her voice as she looked me up and down again.

"Um, yes! That's me. I feel like I should be in all whites or something!" I said awkwardly, realizing my identity was already branded on campus.

"I love tennis," said Iman dreamily, not looking at me. "Tiggy, let's hit later!"

"Okay, well . . . see ya," Victoria said coldly, dismissing me. It was as if she'd said *"Scram, new girl!"* I felt embarrassed and outsidery, clearly not wanted in their vicinity. Not that I really cared. I wasn't coming to Van Pelt to be the equivalent of homecoming queen: I wanted to nail my classes and kick butt on the courts and get into a top university. While the lounge was stunning, I really had zero desire to socialize there and waste time. I was at Van Pelt to excel.

I didn't dare ask Sofia about them until we were in my room with the door closed.

"So, are those, like, the power clique people?" I said, trying to be funny and sarcastic.

Sofia's smile widened into a big grin. She nodded. The ice was broken. Each school I went to, I knew the drill. There was always a pretty posse that ruled the school.

"You got it. They're called the Diamonds. Everyone knows who they are. Antigone is Theodoro Papadapolis's daughter."

My face was blank.

"You know," said Sofia with a slight eye roll. "The billionaire Greek shipping magnate. And Iman is the Princess of Zamumba. You *have* heard of Zamumba, haven't you?"

No. "Yes, of course."

"And Victoria is a Von Hapsburg. I guess a princess or something, but then aren't all those Europeans titled in one way or another?"

"Not any that I know." I was seriously in awe. A princess? *Two* princesses? I'd never mingled with royals. Now some things were starting to make sense: when I sent in my enrollment contracts, I also had to sign a thick document involving silence to the press, to prevent student spies from gabbing about their illustrious classmates.

"We can dish more about them later," Sofia said with a sly wink. "Unfortunately they're in our sectional. So what do you think of your room?"

I had been too preoccupied by the amazing tour (and students straight out of the catalog) to look around fully and take it all in. My room was insane. As big as the house my family lived in when I was little. The furniture was immaculately restored antiques. Oil paintings and scenic watercolors caged in gold frames hung on the walls. The toile curtains framed a window that looked out on the picturesque Swiss Alps. And what was most amazing was that, unlike my classmates, I hadn't flown in a decorator to custom appoint the room; it had been left as is by my predecessor, the student who had lived in it the previous year. She'd breezed out of there leaving every last curtain tassel. I guess since it had been all made specifically for this room, she didn't need it when she left. I drank it all in, still shocked I was even there. But right at that moment, what was beckoning me was the king-size bed that loomed in the corner, with fluffy white sheets and a giant cashmere throw draped across the end. I just wanted to dive in and sleep, sleep, sleep.

Sofia seemed to notice I was tired, so she gave me a small hug.

"Listen, do not let those wretched beeyotches get you down," she instructed. "Now rest up and come knock on my door when you're up to it. You're going to love it here, promise!" She smiled. She headed for the door and then turned back to me at the last second. "And, dahling, don't worry about the whole scholarship thing. My lips are sealed."

Chapter Three

The blood slowly ran out of my face.

"Um . . . yeah. So much for confidentiality on the financial aid form," I stammered, trying to laugh it off. But inside I was livid. The fact that I was on a full ride was not need-to-know info for my fellow students; I suddenly felt branded as the bum of Van Pelt.

"Hey, don't fret, dahling," she said. Her voice had the regal diction of Queen Elizabeth herself. For all I knew, they were related. I could sense already from her tour that everyone there was all two degrees apart from a throne. It was like the Kevin Bacon game but with royals.

"Well, it's just strange having everyone know my situation," I said, focusing on her shoes: five-inch peep-toe pumps.

"They don't," she said, glossy lips pursing into a Cameron-Diaz-meets-Cheshire-Cat smile. "I simply make it my business to know *every*thing about *every*body. I have my spies. But I like you, Wimbledon. You seem very observant to me. And sharp. You know, a lot of kids here don't give a hoot about academics—it's all about the next social event."

"Yeah, well, I'm not incredibly social. I mean, I'd like to be, in some ways, since this is my first school where I'll actually have time to forge a social life, but I'm really here to do well in class and play tons of tennis. And quite frankly, even if I wanted to gel with everybody, I'm not sure they'd be into me, without my ponies and all," I joked.

"Don't worry," she comforted me. "No one will ever know you don't have a billion like everyone else here. Your secret's safe with me."

"It's not that I want to be secretive about my scholarship . . . I just don't want it advertised," I said. "So, how do you know so much after just one year here?" I asked.

She let out a throaty laugh like an opera singer I'd seen on TV, head thrown back dramatically, red lips parted. "Oh! Dahling," she said, coming to sit on my bed beside me, "I am practically the eyes and ears of Van Pelt! In one year I've already harvested the dirt on every priss who strolls these hallowed halls. Don't forget, I'm in the Golden Key Club. I give tours to new students but also to prospective applicants, so not only am I wandering the campus all day, I also have access to everyone's files. Stick with me and I'll show you the ropes, as it were."

"Is there a lot of dirt to be had?" I asked curiously. I was semi-fascinated. I couldn't believe Sofia admitted to being such a snoop! I kind of liked it, though. Even if I was here to score a kick-ass college spot, I was intrigued by the world I'd been plunged into, and clearly she knew every last detail about it.

"These people live the most extraordinary lives—you can't imagine."

I liked the way she drew out the word *extraordinary*, as if it were twenty syllables. She had edge. I could listen to her English accent for hours, and had a feeling I would. I could tell we had the potential to be friends—she had a fun, confident way about her, and no one else was exactly running up to meet the new chick. While we were quite different, her warm yet mischievous grin was a comfort.

"I feel like I'm at the U.N. and I'm the McDonald's-eating American," I confessed.

"Rubbish!" she snapped, patting my head. "There's another American, some Texan. Oh! And a Rolling Stones offspring who was raised bicontinental—London and New York. Don't worry. You'll adore it here! There's a crop of positively delicious new guys, and I watched the whole lot of them approach Le Chambord last evening. We'll get you settled in with some lovely lad who would simply love to get all caught up in your tennis net, so to speak!"

She winked.

I blushed.

While I won't pretend she hadn't read my mind, it was odd to dive in so quickly to the topic of the opposite sex. Due to my rigorous tennis schedule, I hadn't dated since I had split from a mini-relationship on the base. Since then, life had been a whirlwind of three-hour daily practices at each of my schools, travel to tournaments every weekend, and morning workouts. Not a ton of time to fall in love.

But while the tour of Van Pelt's vast grounds intimidated me, it had planted several seeds of hope as I noticed many a hot charmer strolling by. Wait: *Lucy, cut it out!* I told myself. *You are here for academics and tennis.* With a lame average, my scholarship would poof away like these kids' platinum card bills, and while they could spend hours studying, I had to be on the courts; I could not get distracted by the allure of some British lord or Spanish equestrian.

"Hold on a second." Sofia disappeared out of my room while my mind insisted on wandering. How cool would it be to hook up with a royal? Or the child of a rock star? Although my parents would be less than thrilled with the latter. They were really strict, and my father absolutely recoiled when he saw anyone with long hair or even the smallest tattoo. I scratched the rocker from my fantasies.

"Here," said Sofia, returning to my room and tossing a pile of European social magazines like *OK!* and *HELLO!* on my bed. "These are practically a facebook for Van Pelt. Have a gander before you crash in that bed of yours." She smiled with a wink, patted my head, and wished me good night. I reclined into my fluffy pillow and picked up one of the magazines, looking at the glossy pictures from the Crillon international debutante ball in Paris, where all the girls were clad in couture, their escorts in white-tie and gloves. While I was happy to at least gab with Sofia, I was beginning to worry that she might be the *only* one I could relate to—the camera-ready perfection of the classmates I spied in the magazines kind of made me feel like I could never live up to the Van Pelt standard of beauty. I'd always been told I was pretty, but I know I'm the gal-on-the-tennis-court kind of pretty, not the Paris runway knockout. My thoughts made me weary and my eyelids began to close, and the oversize, vibrantly colored magazine slipped to the floor.

Chapter Four

I awoke to the sound of a violin. As my eyes fluttered open in a sublime, warm, cozy state of peace, I realized that the strings I heard were from a *live* violin. I'd forgotten that on my tour yesterday one of the things I'd learned was that violin prodigy Rioko Watanabe from Kyoto was in residence next door, complete (natch) with a million-dollar Stradivarius for performances that Daddy had bought her at auction at Doyle New York.

As I lay there drinking in my view of the Swiss Alps and listening to the rich sounds of Rioko's music, I realized how lucky I was. "This is a wonderful opportunity for you," my mother had said. "Even with the scholarship, it's still costing us an arm and a leg to get you there and back, so don't mess it up," my dad had said. Everyone was rooting for me. I had to try and do my best and appreciate every moment.

I glanced down on the floor where the magazine had fallen. The page was open to a photograph I hadn't seen the previous night. I didn't have to read the caption to recognize who it was: Prince Oliver, the young second cousin of William and Harry who was really like their brother. He was also the Duke of Wickham and had been launched into the media when he suddenly had become a star tennis player last season. The world not only took notice but also embraced him—his movie-star looks and down-to-earth vibe (there were photos of him walking his golden retriever down a London street, playing in the field with his baby niece, etc.) had catapulted him onto the must-watch royal lists, along with the Monaco children and the Swedish princesses.

After gazing at the photo of him cheering on his father in a polo game in the spread, I was shocked to read the caption: *Prince Oliver leaves Bath next week to return to Van Pelt.* No wonder the school had such strict privacy rules. But I could tell already that no one at Van Pelt would dare gossip to the royal chasers. These students didn't need the money, first off, and second, that would just be sooo . . . beneath them. This was a class-act kind of establishment.

I turned the page, hoping for more glimpses of Oliver, but instead found another human of cinema-caliber looks: Angelina de Brulen. Her moon-shaped face was accented by high cheekbones and ice blue eyes. In the photograph she wore a diamond tiara and white gown. She was listed in the caption as the Viscountess of Luxembourg. I wasn't even quite sure what that title was, but as I'd learned in the previous twenty-four hours, there's some kind of royal family for every infinitesimal strip of land. And that family sends its children to Van Pelt.

After I finally hauled my limp bod out of that dangerously comfortable bed, I showered in my marble bathroom (which was nicer than the bathrooms of any hotel I'd ever stayed in) and got dressed with the excited, nervous energy only a new student can feel. What lay outside my door was a mystery, and until I got on those tennis courts, I knew my racing heart would not cease.

I opened the door and walked to the room next to mine. A small plaque read SOFIA GLENN. I knocked, and her Elizabethan accent chirped a friendly "Come in!"

Her room looked cut and pasted from a château but still had hip touches—framed vintage rock-and-roll posters, a basket with piles of designer sunglasses, and an open closet filled with amazing threads (even if they were way too skimpy and bright for my taste).

"Lucy, dear!" she exclaimed, looking at my reflection as she held two potential outfits up to her skinny, toned body in a full-length gilt-framed mirror.

"Thanks for the mags. You're right, they are like facebooks for the school. . . . "

"Did you see that Angelina de Brulen?" she said, rolling her eyes.

"Yes. She's gorgeous. Wait, does she go here?"

"Yes. But just for a semester. Van Pelt has a Swiss semester program where you can sign up for a term here. Some students use it as an audition to see if they like it before they commit. That way if they can't handle it and pull out, it doesn't look like they are dropouts. Hopefully Miss Angelina will stay."

"You want her to stay?" I wondered.

"Oh, you know," she said coyly. "It's just so much more fun having a big high-profile heiress around. It's like every day is the Oscars. Red carpets all around."

I could see how having the pages of those magazines pop to life in the hallways or cafeteria would make for some good people watching. Which even non-scenesters like me could appreciate.

"Come on, let's go get our class schedules." Phew. Actual classes and stuff to do beyond gaping at our stellar constellation of famous classmates! I could see how all the glamour could be a distraction to some. But not me. I would be 100 percent focused.

Sofia guided me through the main courtyard into a small building with marble pillars. A discreet gold sign in French told me it was the registrar's office. On the way we saw dozens of chicly clad students greeting one another, obviously happy to be reunited after a summer of yachting and sunbathing in far-flung exotic locales. I envied the ease with which they laughed and talked, and couldn't wait until I felt fully immersed and able to do the same with a few more friends of my own.

The office had plush wall-to-wall carpeting and French antiques, enormous dark wood pieces behind which sat stern-looking Frenchwomen. They were all polished and chic in that European way, with very tailored suits and hair swept back neatly from their faces, but I kind of wished one of them would crack a smile. Sofia got her registration packet and plopped down on the settee to read through her class schedule. After I said my name, the woman behind the desk told me to wait a minute and disappeared into a back room. Seconds later, she reappeared and motioned for me to follow her. I shot Sofia a nervous look, but she mouthed *Go for it* so I followed the lady, who led me into an office with a middle-aged man in a business suit typing on his computer.

He smiled and motioned for me to sit down.

"Welcome to Van Pelt, Miss Peterson," he said. "I am Monsieur Chival, the academic dean. We are so glad to have you."

"Thank you," I said timidly.

"How do you like Van Pelt so far?"

"It's amazing, I can't believe I'm here, I'm so excited. . . . " I said, my voice trailing off.

The man nodded. "Good, good. Miss Peterson, I have here your academic packet, which includes your courses and such. We assigned you Monsieur LeComte as your advisor. I think you will find him to be a wonderful guide as you begin your journey here. And there is information about your tennis team. Coach Sachs is eagerly waiting to see you again. Says you're quite a star in the making. We're very lucky to have you here, Miss Peterson."

Them lucky to have *me*? I blushed. I was starting to feel better. Maybe through my tennis I'd have a chance to fit in and make friends. Things were all starting to come together. I hoped.

Chapter Five

"You're late," said the man in a brusque German accent two courts away. I recognized Coach Sachs, a lanky man in his midforties with a thick mass of salt-and-pepper hair. I could feel the blood rise to my face as I picked up my pace.

"I am?" I called meekly.

"You were supposed to be here one hour ago, Miss Peterson. It's on the schedule black as black. We've been loitering about waiting for you."

I felt nauseous. I looked around at the twenty faces staring at me curiously from across the clay tennis court. One I recognized as Victoria, a member of the Diamonds. She had a haughty, arrogant look on her face, and she blew a stray hair out of her eyes in irritation. Next to her, on the baseline, was a thin guy about my age with bright red hair and a freckled complexion. He eyed me with curiosity. I gulped when I realized that standing across the net, in an immaculate white tennis outfit with the word PRADA across it, was none other than Angelina de Brulen, who appeared even more gorgeous and intimidating in person. She gazed at me evenly. Way in the back were other girls retrieving balls, and more members of the boys' team were on the adjacent court.

"I can't have lateness on my team," said the coach. He had been much warmer when we'd met in Brussels at my tennis tournament. Now he seemed angry and frustrated by my tardiness. So much for Chival saying Sachs was eagerly awaiting my arrival.

As I looked down, ashamed, I caught Victoria staring at me with a weirdly satisfied, bitchy grin on her face. What was her problem? Ugh. How could I have been late? I was so careful. I had pored over the schedule, which said that tennis starts at ten on Mondays. . . . Great. I'd already messed it all up, got everyone to hate me, and I had only been here two days.

"I'm so sorry. I had no idea. . . . "

"Don't let it happen again. I do not like it. Here to the left is Assistant Coach Albright and Sub-assistant Coach Clement. Liliana and Katrine are our ball girls. Suki and Heather are the trainers. Emme is the massage therapist." I eyed the uniformed staff clad in burgundy zip-up suits with the Van Pelt crest; they almost outnumbered the actual team. "All right, line up, then, we're doing drills."

"Tough luck, Lucy," a snide teasing voice said. I turned to see Victoria jogging by to the other side of the court. Ah, torture the new gal. I got it.

I sprinted over to the line and found I was next to Angelina.

"Hi," I said softly. "I'm Lucy Peterson."

"Angelina," she replied in a businesslike tone, turning back to the net to prepare for one of the coach's lobs. I felt myself redden even more. I was so riled up by Victoria that I missed the first shot, and I could feel Victoria's smirk burn in my side. Focus, Lucy. By my second time I was able to slice a shot across the net that grazed Victoria's thigh and then went past her. Who's smirking now?

"We're not out to hurt our teammates, Peterson. Keep it civil." shouted the coach.

Again my face burned. Was everyone against me?

"She's just got a wicked shot, coach," said the redheaded boy. Thanks! Chivalry is not dead! "But she hits like a guy," he added, deflating my opinion of him at once. In tennis strength is usually thought of as a good thing, but the way he said it let me know he was somehow dissing me.

The coach had us line up and do speed shots, where we hit the ball then ran around to the other side. The drills lasted an hour, and I was wiped out. Angelina and Victoria were good, but it was clear that I was better. I thought I'd have some serious competition, given the illustrious program Van Pelt offered, but it seemed all the private coaches and custom tennis outfits couldn't beat natural talent. I really wanted to be top seed on the team. Sure, they had all the fancy rackets and outfits, but when it came to shots I was superior, even as a sophomore. At least that knowledge cheered me a little.

"Water break," announced Coach Sachs before he beelined into the clubhouse.

Everyone else walked over to the water cooler on the side of the court, so I assumed that we were meant to bake in the still-boiling September sun while Coach got to relax in the shade. Nice. Clearly he took a page from the school's unwritten diva book.

I waited at the end of the line to get my chilled bottled spring water. As soon as Angelina took her two bottles, she walked off to the side of the court to stretch next to a guy who seemed very good-looking from afar. From the way she handed him a water, they appeared to be a couple. Victoria immediately followed, and I watched them curiously. It would make sense that Victoria and Angelina were friends, since they probably moved in the same circles outside of school.

"So, you're the newbie," said the redhead, more as a fact than a question. "My name's Maxwell."

"Hi, yes. I'm Lucy. The new girl."

"Where are you from?" he asked.

"Well, I'm American, but my parents live in Germany."

"Bankers?"

"No. Foreign service."

"Your dad the ambassador?" asked Maxwell, perking up. I guess my dad's nonillustrious occupation was a rarity.

"Um, not quite," I said. "So is this the entire team?" I added quickly.

"Naw, just the sophomores. Each grade practices among themselves."

"Oh," I replied, and then Sachs came out of his office.

"Team! Ten minutes left to break!" he barked, holding up his stopwatch before returning inside.

"Gosh, it's hot today, bloody torture," said the guy who had been sitting with Angelina. He walked up and stood next to Maxwell. I was stunned. It was *Prince OLIVER*. And if he had seemed hot in his picture in the magazine? *Hotter!* It was like a gust of romantic wind slapped me in the face. Seriously. He was tall and in shape, was still tanned from the summer, and had golden flecks in his brown hair. He had piercing blue eyes that crinkled in the corners, and eyebrows that were just a little bit darker than his hair color, which I found to be so hot. All of a sudden the workout and the heat made me feel a little dizzy.

"Yeah." *Yeah?* That's all I could say? Pathetic.

"I'm Oliver," he said, sticking out his hand.

"Prince Oliver," added Maxwell in a snotty tone.

"Max, cut it out," said Oliver, sounding embarrassed.

"I'm Lucy."

"You're a darn good tennis player," said Oliver. "Saw you out there," he said, nodding to the clay court. "Killer volleys."

"Thanks," I said. Okay, why did I have to get so red? I must have looked like a burn victim, seriously, because my face was on fire. Had I never talked to a boy before?

"Look, she's blushing!" Maxwell pointed out the obvious. Jerk.

"She's not blushing; it's just a million degrees out here," said Oliver gallantly.

"Oliver! Angelina just told me the funniest story. Come here!" shouted Victoria from the bench across the court.

"I want to hear it!" shouted Maxwell, dragging Oliver over to the girls. I watched as Oliver plopped down next to Angelina and leaned against her.

I stood frozen by the water cooler, mortified. I wasn't invited across court to hear the hilarious story, so I looked like a complete tool. I pretended I needed more water, and when that didn't kill enough time I became very involved with rewrapping the tape on my racket as if my life depended on it. I could hear the laughs and chatter from the little gang and felt wildly insecure and out of place. I couldn't wait for Coach to return, and almost as though he could feel me willing him, he made his entrance.

"Okay, now, we'll practice the serves," commanded Coach, clapping his hands furiously.

We lined up and each took a turn. Victoria's ball landed in the net. Angelina had a weak serve that made it over the net and in place but without any power. Oliver was pretty good, but

Maxwell slammed across the net in the best effort of the day so far. When it was my turn I took a deep breath and whacked the ball. It landed perfectly in the corner, slicing over the net. I beamed. This was where I excelled.

"Good shot, Peterson," said Sachs. "But we have to do something about that racket. It's as old as Chris Evert." He exited, his massive staff in tow.

"Oh my God!" Victoria squealed, looking down at my hand. "You're going to need to buy a racket that was made in the twenty-first century. I mean, helloooo, that's like one step above those wooden ones!"

And with that, my day was ruined.

Chapter Six

"Um, this seat is saved," said Antigone, putting her hand out so that Sofia and I couldn't sit down at their table.

"Saved? All five seats are saved?" demanded Sofia.

"Yes, for *friends*," said Antigone, who then turned back to Iman and Victoria and laughed. It was so childish, it was insane.

"Fine," said Sofia, whisking up her tray and walking over to another table. I followed.

"I would never have even *tried* to sit there, Sofia," I said, embarrassed.

"Why not? They don't own the lunchroom," she said, slamming down her tray.

"But it's clear they are not interested in being friends with us," I said.

"My relatives are just as royal as theirs," she huffed. "I couldn't give a rat's arse about them, anyway."

I watched Sofia as she took a sip of her steaming skim latte, perfectly frothed by the professional baristas who worked in the school cafeteria ("Cocoa or cinnamon on that?"). Clearly she had a thorn in her side about the Diamonds. I mean, I wasn't into them either, but she seemed more undone by their bitchiness.

It was my fifth day at school, and I felt like I was getting into some semblance of a groove. I finally knew where my classes were, I knew when to get to practice (I hadn't been wrong; Oliver told me that despite the schedule saying practice is at ten, we're supposed to get there at *nine*.) I knew the social ladder, and I clearly wasn't at the top. The Diamonds seemed to be the clique that everyone wanted to get into. They were the most confident, the most decked out, and in a way the prettiest. Not really individually, but as a collective. However, though they might rule the roost as a group, the person that everyone—including them—wanted to be friends with was definitely Angelina, the Queen Bee. She remained aloof. It was not that she was unfriendly; she just kind of kept her distance. She wouldn't have bothered me at all, except for the fact that it was clear Oliver was into her. He was really the only one she talked to, and I saw them now and then having deep conversations. Not that I could ever get a guy like him, but it was a bummer to have him taken.

We settled into our table across the room and started to eat our pasta. I had only taken a bite of my macaroni and cheese with shaved white truffles when Sofia got to her favorite topic.

"So what did Angelina wear today?" she asked. She was as obsessed with Angelina as everyone else, and she made me give daily reports on her outfits at tennis.

"I don't know, white!"

"You're pathetic. Was it designer?"

"There was a little interlocking *C* and *D* on her warm-up jacket."

"Hello? Christian. Dior. Nice. I didn't know they made tennis clothes, though they probably don't. Just for her. What about her jewelry?"

"We're not allowed to wear jewelry."

"Not even earrings?"

"I don't know," I admitted.

"You're so cute, Lucy. You'll learn!"

Just then Victoria and Iman walked past our table.

"Nice pants, Evert!" Victoria sneered, looking down at my plain black pants. They giggled conspiratorially and walked off. Pathetic. I wanted to not care, but why did they have to be mean?

"What's that about?" asked Sofia.

I filled her in on Coach Sachs's mockery of my racket, which seemed to have further fueled Victoria's juvenile teasing.

"He should be one to talk, since before he worked at Van Pelt he manned a second-rate gym in East Berlin," said Sofia, again displaying her knowledge of everyone's backstory. "But those slags should really shut their mugs!" she said icily.

I sighed. "What can I say? I'm no fashion plate."

"That's true, love," she said, but then, seeing my look, quickly added, "but I can help you."

"How? I can't revolutionize my wardrobe with my stipend."

"Yes you can! I can give you some tips, like a fun makeover," she said, leaning back and assessing me.

"I don't think so . . . ," I began, but my voice faltered.

"You're sooo pretty, dahling! Really, your face and bod, you could be a knockout. You just . . . don't have experience with this, is all. And some makeup could work wonders. And highlights!"

I found myself touching my light brown hair. "I was blond as a baby," I said, trying to joke.

I had thought of myself as a somewhat together person who was smart enough and athletic enough to get into this school and go off, away from her parents and sister, and try to make life better. And now I felt like the Gap had thrown up on me while everyone else was in Milan's latest.

"Why do you think they hate me?"

"They don't hate you," said Sofia. "Victoria's just threatened because she was always number one on the tennis team and word is that you might replace her."

Really? She was? Still, that was no way to behave. "But why do they all have to be nasty?"

"They stick together like glue. They know they have more power as a pack. Listen, they're going to make your life hell if they think you have something they want, which you do: your tennis skills. These girls are used to getting whatever they want. They're all like Veruca Salt from *Charlie and the Chocolate Factory*. I just want you to be prepared."

"Great, I feel so much better," I said, a bite of macaroni stuck mid-esophagus.

"But don't worry about those hos," Sofia comforted, with a hand on my arm. "One way to do it is to not give them any unnecessary ammunition. So if you ever want to raid my closet, you're more than welcome." Somehow her English accent relaxed me à la Julie Andrews as Mary Poppins or Maria von Trapp. Thank goodness I had Sofia.

But despite Sofia's soothing words, when I got back to my room I collapsed on my bed and hot tears came rushing out in a bout of homesickness. All I wanted now were my family and to be home in my tiny house on the base. I grabbed the princess phone on the desk and dialed.

"Hello?" It was Amanda, my big sister! Finally someone to show me some love.

"Mandy! I'm so bummed," I said, my voice choking.

"Hey, what's wrong?" she asked sympathetically.

When I had finally calmed down enough to fill her in on the details—the insensitive comments by Coach and the random meanness of the Diamonds—there was silence on the other end of the phone.

"Macaroni and cheese with white truffles?" she asked. "Don't truffles cost like five hundred dollars?"

"I guess," I said, wiping my nose with my shirt. "But that's not the point. I just miss you guys. It's very intense here."

"Yes it is the point, Lucy. I mean, yeah, it sucks that the girls are bitches, but what did you expect?"

"Well . . . I . . . just thought they wouldn't be so harsh," I sputtered in surprise.

"Well, life is harsh. And I'm sorry that those girls are snotty, but grow up. You've told me about your giant bedroom with the plasma TV and the amazing food and the cool classes you get to take, like International Waters Law and Dissection of Fairy Tales, and you're like, hobnobbing with royalty, and then you cry 'cause one girl tells you that you need to dress better? Give me a break."

"You don't understand. . . ."

"No I don't. And unfortunately I won't. Because you were the lucky one who got to go there. Me? I had to sign up for ROTC to pay for college, so one day I could be shipped out to God knows where while you'll get a tennis scholarship if you play your cards right. Suck it up, sis," she said, slamming down the phone.

I sat there in shock, holding the silent phone. I couldn't believe Amanda had hung up on me! I wanted to cry, but I took deep breaths to calm myself down as I thought about what she had said. I *was* lucky. Sure, these girls were nasty and snobby, but

I was here for myself. I just needed to keep my head down, get a great education, go to a stellar college, and make something of myself. Stay the course, as my dad would say.

Taking another deep breath to pull myself together, I stared at myself from every angle of my giant three-way mirror and realized that maybe, just maybe, I *could* use a little touch-up. I could never wear short skirts or big jewelry, but maybe it could be fun to be a tad more girly.

Chapter Seven

I walked down the hall toward Sofia's room and was about to knock when I heard something odd.

I couldn't quite believe my unpierced ears. My hand hovered by the gold knocker on Sofia's door as I held my breath. I knew the difference between the sound of a TV and a live speaking voice, and what I distinctly heard was Sofia's voice—the exact tone and cadence—but with an altogether different accent. Gone was the clipped, perfect, lilting chirp of the queen or her great-nephew Prince Oliver. In its place? Two words: Oliver Twist.

My lungs filled instantly with a rush of air at the realization: Sofia had been affecting an accent! She really spoke in thick street-urchin cockney. It couldn't be.

"Awl right, awl right!" she snapped into the phone. Her words sounded completely different. "Oy am doeen me best!" I heard the phone slam down. I stepped away from the door, letting go of the knocker gently.

I heard Sofia clear her throat. Then, in a magic millisecond, she flicked her aristocratic aura back on and out came her *other* English. "Is someone there?" She said *there* in her singsongy, charming and precise British manner, a far cry from the "Bri-ish" pickpocket-ese I'd heard only a moment before.

I panicked. "Um . . . Sofia? Hi! I was . . . just walking by—" Stupid! Ugh. Okay, Lucy, play dumb.

The door whipped open. Sofia stared at me skeptically, eyelids at half-mast. "How long were you out there?" she said, studying me as she awaited my answer.

"No time at all!" I stammered. "Um, just was walking by and I heard the phone hang up. I was hoping you were free to get a snack . . . I'm starving."

She leaned on her door frame, her tall, lithe body draped in a fancy lace-trimmed silk robe. She folded her arms and squinted her eyes. My body quietly shook as I felt like a defendant about to hear a jury's verdict.

"Okay," she said slowly. "I'll come. I'm hungry as well." *Phew.*

We went to Caffè VP, one of the four on-campus restaurants

(with menus in seventeen different languages and currencies), and I practically deserved an Oscar for my performance. It was as if I still thought of her as my posh neighbor slash budding friend who I looked up to to show me the ropes. Only now I knew she was hiding something from me. I listened attentively as she identified the crowd of beautiful people, each bedecked with a different set of logos and bling.

"There goes Leigh Ofer. She is one of the coolest girls in school. Her boyfriend graduated last year, and he's one of the top polo players in Argentina. That's Fifi von Fabercastel from Germany—her uncle makes every eyeliner in the world. Oh, and there's Shyla LeCreuze. She's from Belgium, and her dad invented chocolate."

"Um . . . I think the ancient Mayans invented chocolate as we know it—," I carefully corrected.

"Whatever. He's major in the chocolate world. When you say 'Belgian chocolates' you're talking about them." As she studied everyone around us, I simply studied her. The way she said "Whatever" was more like "Wha-eva," with tiny peeks of the Dickensian cockney shining through. *What was her deal?* Why the smoke and mirrors reflecting a moneyed and socially connected life when she was talking to someone as decidedly unglam as me? I was curious. I didn't quite know what to think let alone say, so I remained quasi-mute for the rest of lunch. I had to play it very safe here—she was my only friend so far, and I couldn't let on that I knew. I needed a sure-footed strategy. She was the quick jackrabbit type who ran up to the net to swat volleys dramatically, and I would be the one slowly swinging at the baseline, soberly returning shot after shot after shot.

Chapter Eight

The next day, after lobbing steady shots at Sofia in the social game of tennis, I hit the actual courts for practice. Though I knew I was kicking arse in my game (Coach Sachs even thawed for a moment and yelled "Yessss!" after one of my aces, pumping his arm dorkily), I was weirdly self-conscious when Oliver was assigned to the court next to mine. Obviously all girls swooned in his royal presence, but what disarmed me so much was his casual smile and relaxed, athletic demeanor—especially compared to his pal Maxwell's cocky swagger.

43

"Hey, Venus!" Maxwell teased as I headed to the Evian cooler.

"Oh, hi," I said, brushing my hair out of my face.

Oliver had already grabbed two Evians. Maxwell reached out his sweaty arm toward the H_2O, but Oliver dodged him as a huge grin flashed across his face. "Ladies first."

To my shock, he handed me the bottle, customized with the VP crest. "Thanks," I said, my blush mercifully disguised by my pink sweaty cheeks.

"See, we Euros know how to treat a lady," Maxwell said at the same time he checked out my legs.

"Most of us," Oliver corrected, giving me a look as if to say he got the fact that his friend was a semi–a-hole.

"Well I guess that's why they call it the Old World," I said, feeling awkward. "But the charm is not lost on me. Thanks again."

Then I saw Angelina watching from two courts down. Uh-oh. Sorry to crash the royal parade.

"Hi, boys," Victoria chirped, strutting over to grab her water sans acknowledgment of my existence.

"Tor," said Maxwell, looking her over. "How are we doing today?"

"Oh, you know, lovely. Tiggy and Iman and I are going to meet up later, you guys should come—"

Angelina approached the group as I zipped up my bag and gathered my stuff.

"Oh, Angelina, you must join us!" added Victoria.

My cheeks flushed as I was so clearly being excluded.

"Oh, perhaps I will, thanks," said Angelina noncommittally. She was being her incredibly polished, polite self, but still reserved and aloof, making me think she wasn't planning on becoming the fourth Diamond.

Back in the dorm I was eager to tell Sofia of my interaction, because she was still my only (kind of) friend, even though I knew she was hiding who she was from me for whatever reason. Maybe because this school was such a pressure cooker of social hierarchies, she felt compelled to mask her "common" background. Luckily—hand to God—I didn't really give a damn enough to let it truly get to me, beyond the occasional sting. My tennis would keep me centered on my goal. And while a fun crush on Oliver put a spark in my step, it definitely didn't blur my focus. No matter who he was.

Sofia was nowhere to be found so I ordered room service and got in bed with my history of the Olympics textbook. While Van Pelt was purported to be the top academy in Europe, I must say, my workload was hardly the stress crunch I had experienced in Germany. Some of the classes were actually *easy*. I had assumed that the academics were rigorous, but when I mentioned this to Sofia she said that they had to have tons of "gut classes"—aka easy classes—so that all the royals could ace them and the parents would keep giving lots of dough to the school. Supposedly the parents only cared about excellence on the sports teams or about marital matches—academics came in second. Sofia described it more as "a finishing school where none of the students finished anything." However, in order to keep up their reputation, they recruited several students like me every year to balance out the GPAs and the college acceptances. Hey, if I could be pinned as a token brainiac, all the better. I was there to secure my future, and unlike my classmates, I had no connections to get me into a top college.

As I closed my book and started to close my eyes, I heard a knock on my door. It was Sofia.

"Hi, come in!" I said, genuinely happy to see her. "I was looking for you. Where have you been?"

"I have to talk to you," she said, her normally smiley face dead serious. "Lucy, I have a weird feeling that you know my secret. I have to explain."

Chapter Nine

I brought Sofia into my room, and we both sat down in the large fluffy armchairs by the roaring fire. I felt nervous, even though it was really Sofia who should have been nervous.

"First off, I want to commend you. You're a brilliant actress," said Sofia, giving me a sly smile.

"Um, what do you mean . . . ?"

She waved her hand in the air to cut me short. "You're a brilliant actress, but I am even better. You were quite a bit different at lunch yesterday. Barely said a word. So I guessed you heard me on the telephone."

I nodded, saying nothing.

Sofia sighed deeply and flipped her stick-straight hair behind her shoulder. "The truth is, Lucy, I am not very different from you."

She stared at me evenly and continued.

"I don't come from a rich family, and you heard my accent—I tawk more like Eliza Doo-little than Lady Diana." As she spoke she morphed her voice in an imitation of a poor and then a posh accent.

"So . . . why do you fake it?" I asked.

"I—" She began to confess but then stared at me carefully, her eyes boring through me like laser beams. "I need to know if I can trust you, Lucy."

"You can trust me."

"No, I mean, *really* trust you."

"Okay. I swear, Sofia."

"And swear on the person closest to you that you won't tell anyone. *Anyone.*"

I hate doing that. But okay. "Sure."

"I come from a middle-class family."

"That's nothing to be ashamed of," I began.

"Wait. My mother is a teacher"—she said the last word with contempt—"and my father is a reporter."

"Sofia, those are both admirable professions. I don't think you have any reason to be embarrassed. I mean, I know we're surrounded by kids whose parents are basically God, but it shouldn't really matter. We're here to get an education."

"Lucy, I feel like there's something very trustworthy about you and that you get it and get the scene here. You're the first person I've met who may understand. See, *I'm* not here to get an education," said Sofia, a wicked smile forming on her lips.

"You're not?"

"I'm here to help my dad. You see, he's not just a reporter. He's a top editor at *Gab!* magazine—you know, that monthly glossy that covers celebs and socialites."

"Uh-huh . . . " I pictured the stacks of magazines she'd lent me the evening I'd arrived.

"My dad and his editors cooked up this whole scheme for me to come here as an undercover reporter. They invented this fake background, bought some title off the internet. And the publisher is paying my tuition. All I have to do is supply them with as much gossip as possible every month."

I was stunned. That was so . . . devious.

"Look, before you get judgmental, hear me out," she continued. I hugged the pillows in my arms closer, as if they were a shield that could protect me from the information she was about to reveal. "The parents of a lot of these kids treat my dad like dirt. All he's trying to do is make a living, and for some reason they refuse to talk to people at his magazine. If he got the scoop from them that, say, Victoria von Hapsburg is anorexic—"

"She is?" I interrupted with horror.

"No. But say she was. Hypothetically. If she told my dad that exclusively, the money he would earn from that scoop would pay

49

for my entire university education. I'm talking huge money."

I pondered that while she continued.

"A while back, my mum had serious pains in her stomach. We didn't have the money to go to the best doctor—my dad wasn't at *Gab!* at the time. Anyway, my father happened to see one of the Spice Girls throw up her dinner in a garbage can outside a restaurant and touch her stomach. He knew then and there that she was pregnant. His publisher printed the story, my dad got paid, and my mum went to a top doctor."

I didn't know what to make of all this.

"I know you're thinking you'd never do this, but you have to understand," said Sofia, resting her hand firmly on my arm. "I only tell stories about the bitchy tarts. And I only report on things that everyone here already knows or that have major *international* importance."

"Like what?"

"Like the fact that Ludmila Khritova, that Russian heiress whose father is about to be indicted on fraud charges in London, has been dating the son of a major British Parliament member. That's really important information. Potentially illegal stuff. They are probably being soft on her dad because of her boyfriend's dad, and her dad is, like, a *criminal.* So you see, Lucy, it's really not so bad. I'm either saving the world or spilling harmless secrets like what kind of hair conditioner Claudia Norwich uses. It's frivolous, really."

"Well . . . " I still didn't know what to think. I would never feel comfortable spying on my classmates. I mean, they might be jerks, but they were only famous because of their parents.

"But I decided to tell you, Lucy, because you are a lot like me. We're outsiders looking in. That's why I knew at once we'd be best friends. I could tell you were so smart. Everyone said you were just here for tennis, but once we chatted I knew that was hardly the case."

"Who said that?" Did they think I was just a dumb jock?

"Everyone," said Sofia, raising her eyebrows.

"That's so frustrating! I just can't win."

"But you can with me! I told my dad all about you, and he thinks you sound really clever. Plus, with your tennis team placement, you'll have a bird's-eye view all the time of some key people the magazine is interested in. Dad even told his publisher, who wants to sign you up."

I saw Sofia glance at me out of the corner of her eye to see how I would react.

"But I told him you weren't interested. You probably get a large stipend and don't need two thousand pounds a month."

"Two thousand pounds *a month*?" I had just received the equivalent of a *three*-thousand-pound-a-month stipend from school, but with the astronomical prices in the gift shop I didn't know how long that would last. I had already almost spent the entire month's amount on tennis equipment that Coach Sachs had *insisted* I get. I could see why people had to be so rich to come to this school. It was beyond expensive.

"That's just starting out. But forget it. Anyway, what I wanted to say is please, please don't tell anyone about my secret, okay?"

I didn't want to be coconspirator, but what good would it do if I told people?

"Okay," I said lamely.

"Thanks, love, I knew I could trust you," Sofia said, leaping up and embracing me.

"Yeah."

I walked her to the door, and just as I was closing it behind her, she put her hand out to stop it.

"You know, Lucy, I think you'd be good at this kind of thing. Think about it."

Before I could answer, she turned and walked down the hall to her room.

Chapter Ten

Over the next few days, I steered clear of discussing Sofia's secret life with her. I thought it better to pretend that we never had our conversation, and thankfully she didn't bring it up. In the meantime, I was still trying to acclimate to school and the increasing demands of the tennis team. Coach Sachs was merciless.

On Wednesday we had a three-hour practice after which I literally thought I would pass out. After we finished, Coach gathered us all around to make some announcements.

"Mediocre work," he said with a frown. "You must try harder. We have a major match coming up next week. I have the roster now. Peterson will play first singles. Von Hapsburg, you're downgraded to second. You have to try harder, run harder, work out more," he said.

I couldn't believe he was berating her in front of everyone. I sneaked a peek at her face, which was frozen in horror. I almost felt bad for her.

"De Brulen, you will be three," he said, pointing to Angelina. "And the boys' placements will remain the same."

With that, he turned and marched off the court. *I'm number one!* I thought gleefully. I was thrilled and also psyched to beat Victoria. I did feel a smidgen bad for her, though. But then I remembered her nasty remarks and didn't feel that bad.

The group got up and started to disperse.

"Congratulations."

I knew the voice but didn't turn around because I assumed he wasn't talking to me.

"Yoo-hoo? You in there?" I felt a tap on my shoulder.

"Huh?" I said, twisting around and coming face-to-face with Oliver.

"Well done," he said with a smile.

"Thanks," I said, noticing Victoria glare at me out of the corner of my eye.

"It was bloody hell out there today! I've never run so many laps around the court." He smiled, flushed from the sprints.

"Yeah, it was brutal."

"I'm exhausted!" said a dewy (not sweaty!) Angelina, who came up with a fresh towel around her neck. She flopped onto Oliver's shoulder. "I feel simply faint! I could drink a river."

"Is that a hint?" said Oliver with a smile. "Okay, chivalry is not dead. I'll get you girls some *agua*."

"I've never felt so out of shape in my whole life," I lamented to Angelina as Victoria came bounding up, her long hair in a twist.

"Oh, please," Victoria said to me sarcastically, eyes squinting. "What bullshit. You're, like, Muscle Girl! It's *much* harder for people with wispier builds like Angelina and me!"

Okay . . . bitch. I know you're upset that you were knocked to number two, but don't take it out on me. And I'm sorry, but I am not the Incredible Hulk or anything. I'm athletic and fit, but not some big bulky Amazon. She made me feel like she and Angelina were willowy waifs while I was some Thor type. "Well, I'm still wiped out," I stammered.

"Right," she said, her voice dripping with sarcasm. She gave me a look, then headed off down the hill, probably back to her safety net of evil friends. The Diamonds seemed like too generous a name for them. Cinderella's Stepsisters would be more appropriate. I watched her ponytail swing back and forth until it was mercifully out of sight.

"Here you go," said Oliver, jogging up with bottles, which he handed to Angelina and me. "Don't ever say I never gave you anything."

I saw Angelina looking at me, and I felt like such a massive idiot. I thanked Oliver and said I had to go back and hit the books.

"You off, then, Lucy? I'll head back with you." He smiled and his eyes had a brightness that, when beamed in my direction, made the ice of Victoria's comment melt away. "What about you, Angelina?" he asked, turning to her.

"I'm going to do some laps on the treadmill. I want to firm up," she said.

"Wow, laps after practice? That's commitment," I said, surprised.

"Yeah" was all she said before saying good-bye and walking away.

"You walking down to the dorms?" asked Oliver, cocking his head to the side and motioning toward campus.

"Yeah."

"Let's go, then," he said.

Oliver was always friendly, but our walk down the hill was the first time he really talked to me. He was usually huddled on the side with Maxwell, a friendship I couldn't figure out because Oliver seemed so nice and Maxwell was so annoying. Sometimes Oliver would talk to Angelina and Victoria, but it always seemed like I was the odd man out. In the beginning I had tried to sort of interact with them, but as the demands of the team got more intense, I was happy to just collapse on the grass whenever we had a break. It was almost easier to keep my distance.

As we walked we made some small talk about the weather and about the coach, and I was amazed that it was so easy to talk to him. Oliver was gorgeous, but the fact that I knew I could never get him, that he would always go for someone like Angelina, actually made me feel relieved. Free, in a way. If I didn't view him as a potential love interest, I could be normal with him. Even with a tiny pitter-patter in my chest.

"So, Lucy, how do you like it here so far?" he asked.

"I like it," I answered. "You know, it's very different from my old school."

"What, you didn't have butlers there? You didn't have Henry Kissinger coming to lecture on peace treaties at your old school?" he joked.

I laughed, refreshed. "No, I'm sorry to say we did not. Mrs. Gramble had to do the peace lectures herself."

"Mrs. Gramble?" Oliver asked, raising his eyebrows in amusement. "That's a name out of a movie."

"I know. She *was* out of a movie. It's called *Return of the Living Dead.*"

"There are some teachers like that here."

"Even here?" I asked, surprised by how playful I was being. "Nawww, can't be!"

"I swear it," said Oliver, putting his hand to chest. "In fact, Napoléon himself teaches here."

"Really?" I said, smiling. "What about Stalin?"

"Yup. And Socrates, Aristotle, and Plato. Van Pelt is the best, so they have to have the best!"

Oliver and I started laughing. It was fun to be silly with him. I was glad he had a sense of humor because most people at the school seemed to take themselves so seriously. We approached my dorm, and I could see the Diamonds lounging on the chaises on the patio playing backgammon. Iman saw us first, then nudged Antigone, who in turn alerted Victoria, still in her tennis clothes, and they all stopped and stared.

"All right, then, I'll catch you later," said Oliver quickly before darting away down the path to his dorm. Did he not want to be seen with me? My face felt hot and I knew I was blushing. But I didn't want the Diamonds to think I had been ditched, so I put on a fake smile and said, "Hey," as I passed them.

"You," said Antigone.

I turned around. "Me?"

"Yes," she said, pointing at me. "What's your name again?"

"Lucy."

"Right," she said, eyeing me up and down. "The American."

Okay, she said "American" in the same tone as she would "baby killer" or "pedophile." Clearly not a fan of the ol' U.S. of A.

"Yes, proud to be!" I said, kind of joking, but kind of not. Don't mess with my country, girlfriend.

"What were you talking to Oliver about?" Tiggy demanded.

"Oliver? Um, nothing."

"Nothing?" inquired Victoria with a stern tone.

"Just chatting about Plato and Socrates and Aristotle," I said with a smile.

Antigone's eyes narrowed. She wore so much heavy makeup that it looked as if her face might crack. She was not bad-looking, so it was weird that she caked all that gunk on. I wondered if she had really bad skin that she had to cover up.

"Are you mocking us?" asked Antigone.

"Bad idea," said Iman, shaking her head so that her large gold hoop earrings looked as if they might Frisbee across the yard.

"No, I'm just kidding."

"Lucy," said Victoria, shifting in her seat and smiling as if a bright idea had come to her, "are you going to Jazzmatazz this Saturday?"

"Jazzmatazz? I don't know. I hadn't heard about it."

"Oh, everyone's going. It's *the* event of the week. Wynton Marsalis is playing, and Wolfgang Puck is preparing a small supper."

"That sounds fun."

Victoria gave Antigone a look who in turn gave Iman a look, and then they all faced me and smiled like coconspirators. What was this about?

"One thing you should know, though: it's white-tie," said Victoria finally.

"White-tie?"

"That's one notch more formal than black," said Iman.

"I know that," I snapped, although I hadn't. White-tie?

Obviously these girls knew I had nothing to wear. What was their problem? Were they pissed that I was talking to Oliver? It was clear because of his high profile and insanely good looks they were intrigued by him (who wouldn't be?), but would they be so outright nasty just because I had talked to him?

"Well, thanks for the heads-up," I said.

I brushed past them into the lobby of the dorm and ran splat into Sofia. She was standing there with her arms crossed and had obviously heard everything.

"They're god-awful, aren't they?" she said, more as a statement than a question.

"Yup." They absolutely were.

"Want to play a prank on them?"

Chapter Eleven

"So what high school has a white-tie thing, anyway?" I laughed, flopping on Sofia's bed.

"I know. Can you believe it?" She rolled her eyes, then sat down next to me and rubbed her hands together to hatch her scheme. "So: every formal we have, snotty Victoria wears this diamond charm bracelet her daddy-o gave her between romps with his international mistresses. Each charm represents a different foreign currency: the dollar symbol, the pound, the euro, the yen, the German mark, the Chilean peso, the Indian rupee, the

Macedonian denar, the Belorussian ruble, the Cape Verdean escudo, the Zambian—"

"I get the point," I interrupted.

She just looked at me.

"Okay," I said. "What's the Zambian one?"

"The Zambian kwacha."

"Okay, so . . . she has all these currency symbols dangling on her wrist? Why is that stylish?" I mused.

"I think it means 'We have money in all these countries.' But that's not the point. The point is, it is thoroughly obnoxious, and if we can just take it and snap some photographs—"

"Take it? You mean *steal*. . . . " I said skeptically.

"No no no, just *borrow* it. We could take a photo of it, and it would run everywhere! We get one at the ball with it on her wrist—I have a great hidden cam for that—but we have to get a close-up beforehand."

"But you know there is no taking photographs allowed inside campus buildings," I protested, having memorized the leather-bound and embossed school handbook on my train ride over.

"But they always go off campus after formals. Everyone goes to Club Platinum in the city and gets tables. It's like an after party that lasts all night—when we have formals, curfew is dawn."

"Are you serious? They didn't have that in the handbook!"

"Yeah, they bend the rules. Only for formals."

"*Dawn?* That sounds like a kind of imprecise curfew. How do they measure that, when the rooster cock-a-doodle-doos?"

"Stop worrying about getting in trouble all the time. You're so military!"

I didn't know quite how to take that, but maybe she was right—after a lifetime of doing exactly what I was told, I had never really gone wild. Maybe a prank was just the fun adventure I needed.

After dinner, Iman, Victoria, and Antigone were gathered on the crowded veranda by the fountain. They were standing behind a table that had a huge sign that said BRING BACK BONO and were soliciting everyone who walked by to sign their petition. Apparently Bono had delivered a controversial speech at Van Pelt last year about all of the wealth at our school and how it could save a nation in Africa from starvation, and the administration vowed he would never come back to speak. The Diamonds had taken it upon themselves to "bring him back" and were loving being the center of attention. I watched as they shouted out to senior guys to come over and sign up, and even flirted with some of the younger male teachers. They flipped their hair provocatively and lowered their eyes coyly—they were truly masters at seduction. I could never imagine having the confidence to act like them.

Oliver walked by and said something to them in greeting, and I watched as all three of their faces beamed and they tossed their heads back in a perfectly executed combination of giggles slash hair flips. Tiggy leaned in and whispered something to Oliver, so he bent down and signed the petition. They were so *forward*. As Oliver walked away from their table, he saw me and came by.

"Hey, Luce," he said, his hand slapping my back as if I were a dude. I wilted under his touch. "Killer court time today." He smiled and walked off, en route to the library. I could barely muster a "Thanks." I felt the heat of the Diamonds' gaze upon me as I looked down at my book and the marble table.

Just as Angelina exited the main hall and walked by the tables carrying her textbook for the history of rock and roll, Sofia came up and tapped my arm.

"God, look at them, they make me sick," she said, snarling in the Diamonds' direction. "They are always first to set up kissing booths for charity or 'Donate Old Manolos events' to raise money for the Van Pelt fashion magazine. They always want everyone to know who they are and to remain the center of attention. Shameless," she said.

We watched as some jocks like Morgan Wellington and Moabi LeTroux, the stars of the cricket team, sat near the Diamonds, clearly trying to woo the cutest girls in the school.

"Hello, ladies," Morgan said salaciously.

"Tiggy. Looking good," Moabi added. Someone was clearly hoping to get lucky at Jazzmatazz.

"Hey, Angelina!" Victoria said to Angelina as she passed by. "Come join our cause!"

"Oh, thanks, but I have to study."

"Studying shmudying!" Antigone laughed, flipping her shiny black hair. "Everyone's going down to Caffè VP tonight, you have to come!"

"We'll see," said Angelina noncommittally as she continued on down the path. Sofia and I glanced up from pretending to read our *Constellations and You* textbook. Angelina looked at her watch and picked up her pace. Probably off to a rendezvous with Oliver. Lucky duck.

"Okay, then!" yelled Victoria after her. "We'll all be there at ten o'clock."

It was mysterious to me why the Diamonds were so determined to be Angelina's friend when she clearly couldn't care less about them. They were practically drooling after her every time they saw her, and yet she always remained aloof. It seemed like she didn't need anyone. I had the impression she was either the biggest snob in the universe or dumb as a board. But with Oliver around her so often, I kind of understood: Why would she need anyone else?

"Bingo," Sofia whispered to me.

"Huh?" I asked.

"Did you hear that? The Diamonds will be at the caffè at ten o'clock. That's when we'll make our move."

"Um, okay."

I felt my stomach drop. Was this really a good idea? Could I get arrested?

"Remember what jerks they are. And don't worry, it's harmless fun," said Sofia, as if reading my thoughts.

I glanced over at the girls and inadvertently caught Victoria's eye. Of course she didn't ask me to sign her petition but instead gave me a dirty look. Oh yes, I was in.

Chapter Twelve

As the three-hundred-year-old grandfather clock in the dorm hallway struck ten, the last of our neighbors scampered out, hair blown dry and glossed, naturally decked out and catwalk ready. Even Rioko, the violinist, put down the frigging fiddle for once to go hang out. It was Thursday, after all, and as every posh jet-setter knows, Thursday is the new Friday. Apparently now Friday was more like a Monday—mellow, resting up for the grand-daddy of nights: Saturday. The new Saturday. Or the old one. Well, as the song goes, "Everybody loves a Saturday night."

Jazzmatazz was forty-eight hours away, and while Sofia and I were nervously hovering outside Victoria's door, all I could picture was Oliver macking with gorgeous Angelina. Gosh, her life was truly perfect. But her Luxembourg throne didn't hold a candle to the crowning glory of a guy like Oliver.

"The coast is clear," said Sofia in a dramatic hushed tone, and I suddenly felt all spy movie-ish. I watched her slowly turn the gilded knob to Victoria's suite, and when it creaked ever so slightly I cringed.

"Careful!" I whispered forcefully.

"No one's around," she said, calming me. The door opened and we bolted in. The only word that came to mind was *magical*. The silk drapes, the upholstered headboard bursting with rosebuds and stripes, the lacquered coffee table piled with books, and not one but two armoires for her clothes—as if the huge walk-in closet in every dorm room wasn't enough. I stood motionless while Sofia got down to bidniss and raided drawers. Finally she found a safe.

She punched in numbers on the digital keypad. Presto! It worked: a tiny bulb lit green, a click sounded, and the door opened before my eyes. I was stunned.

"How did you know that?" I asked, shocked.

"Always the birthday. Yawn! I'm the Golden Key Club gal, remember? Everyone's file has their DOB. Runners-up are their parents' yacht's name, the ancestral estate's name, the favorite racing horse's name—the list goes on," Sofia said blithely. "But

Victoria's too boring and predictable for anything interesting."
The safe contained about fifty velvet boxes of every shape and
color and size. As I approached it, shaking, Sofia casually went
through each box, each containing a magnificent piece of fine
jewelry that had no business being outside a bank vault, let alone
in a school dormitory. Each necklace—rubies, emeralds, and, yes,
diamonds—more spectacular than the next. Then Sofia opened a
blue suede box, displaying a racket-emblazoned medal for Female
First Place in a tennis tournament. I was more interested in that
piece than in the glittering assemblage of flickering stones. I ran
my fingers over the gilded prize. Aha! No wonder she hated me so
much! Her parents or someone were rewarding her court success
with jewelry. I doubt they would give her a diamond bracelet for
second place. I could see how that would sting. Meanwhile, Sofia
opened box after box until finally a small black velvet one on the
side revealed the aforementioned charm bracelet, indeed crass and
picture-worthy in its obnoxiousness. The symbol for every country's currency was, as described by Sofia, dangling in multikarat
glory. Sofia expertly laid it out on one of the bigger boxes to make
a plain black background. She then reached down her shirt into
her bra and pulled out a tiny, long, skinny camera and began
snapping away *Mission: Impossible* style.

"Sofia! You have a camera?" I squealed.

"*Shhh!*" she admonished. "Do you want to get us caught?
Shush up and stand guard."

I obediently ran to the door and listened for the *click-clack* of

Manolo Blahnik heels from any stray student who was loserly enough to still be a dorm rat at this peak social hour. Nothing.

Sofia kept snapping and then put the bracelet away and closed the safe. We high-fived and escaped undetected, much to my amazement.

We darted to the Caffè to see everyone in action and walked in to find the Diamonds all carousing with Oliver, and Maxwell, Morgan, and some other guys visually feasting on the girls' décolletage.

"So," Sofia said, one eyebrow arched slyly, "how easy was that?"

I was truly astonished by the speed and simplicity of it all. "Easy as pie," I responded.

"Dad's gonna give me a big bonus for this one," she marveled mischievously. "And don't worry, Lucy, you'll get your cut."

Chapter Thirteen

The thrill of victory wore off at about three in the morning when I woke up in a cold sweat, my heart racing. I couldn't believe what Sofia and I had done. Had I really risked everything just to exact revenge for fifteen minutes on a girl I barely knew?

Come on, Lucy, I told myself. I'd dealt with girls much worse than Victoria. There was Elsa, the daughter of the doctor on our base in Dubai, who for some reason singled me out for all of her vitriol and rage and made my entire time in the Emirates a nightmare. There was Galt, the bulimic, who was in my class in Texas, who used to go on evil tangents after she threw up in the bathroom. She would get up and write down the names of everyone she hated that day on the blackboard, and somehow I made it up there every time. I cried every day of sixth grade. Victoria was a jerk, but she wasn't ruining my life. She was just trying to let me know that I should stay out of her way.

I wished there was someone I could call. As we were in the same time zone as Germany, I knew my sister would be asleep. And frankly I wasn't sure I wanted to talk to her after she'd read me the riot act last time. I had a feeling she would do the same this time. I hadn't lived in Germany long enough to have a true best friend, one who I could call in the middle of the night. In fact, I realized I didn't have a true best friend anywhere in the world except Emma, who I'd spent a year in school with but who'd moved back to California. I could email her, sure, but at the moment I wanted the soothing nature of a friend's voice. It was as if all my contacts were scattered around the globe, inaccessible and orbits away. The dangers of moving around too much. I started to feel sorry for myself and really angry at my parents. Why did they drag me around the globe? Why couldn't we live in one place for a long time? If we did, I wouldn't have jetted off to boarding school. I might have been able to be on a normal tennis team at a normal all-American high school. Did I really have not one friend? For a second I thought of Sofia, but she was the last person I wanted to talk to. I don't know—all had been well, but I was starting to get a weird sense about her. Like, when I was with her all was well and fun, but when I thought about her, I don't know . . . I had been so happy to bond with her that I strayed from my moral compass. I didn't think I could trust her.

I had plopped on the cashmere-covered window seat and was staring out at the darkness. I could see the mountains in the faint moonlight; it all looked so beautiful and calm. I didn't want to give up this experience. Friends or no friends, this was what my reality was. Then why did I have to go along with Sofia? My heart palpitations got more intense. I scanned the room and noticed my mahogany desk, where the gleaming new computer sat proudly. I hadn't yet dealt with setting up my school email account, and in my loneliness, I felt motivated to reconnect with faraway friends, and have the world at my fingertips.

I logged on to VanPeltWinners.com. It was the school face-book, and everyone had been given a professionally designed web page, which had a small bio and anything else we wanted to post, like movie posters or album covers of our favorite artists. It also had a photograph of each student that was taken over the summer (when they were tan) by a professional fashion photographer who was sent to each student's house with his team, which included a makeup artist, hairstylist, and wardrobe consultant. The result was that every student at the school looked like either Kate Moss or Johnny Depp. I think that was what they were going for. The plan was to have everyone look like they could be models so that the school would seem even more exclusive. My page featured a snapshot my mom took of me on a trip to Bruges—big smile, hair flying in the breeze, blue eyes happy. I looked so innocent then, just a year ago. The school web designers also added tennis graphics and the fact that I was on the tennis team.

I hadn't really checked my web page since I'd been at the school, assuming that I wouldn't receive any posts, but I logged on anyway and established my account. I was astonished to find that I had two postings. One was from Rioko, the violinist, who asked me if I had the homework assignment for our Greek Mythology class. Oops, it was from four days ago, so I assumed she had it by now. My bad. I quickly wrote her back apologizing, explaining I hadn't signed on until now. The other post was from someone whose user name was Friend. Hmm . . . interesting. I clicked on the message. It said:

Hey, saw you play tennis today. You're really amazing. I just wanted to say I hope you're having a good time at this school.

That was nice. I wonder who it was? And I wondered why they didn't sign their name? It wasn't a crime to give compliments. In fact, it totally made me feel better.

I quickly wrote a response:

Thanks, mystery friend. I appreciate the compliment. I was feeling majorly down and friendless, and you just cheered me up.

I pressed Send. Why not? Maybe my friend felt the same way? She was probably down the hall from me right now, feeling left out and sad. I wished I knew who she was. I wouldn't think she was a dork at all.

I flipped through the pages of the facebook and found Victoria's. It was so pretentious. She had a picture of her family crest, photos of her castle, a list of her favorite things, which included caviar (barf), summers in Saint Tropez, champagne, and "hanging out with Liz Hurley in Knightsbridge." Gag. She also had a Q&A on there, and to the question "What's your idea of misery?" she answered: "Flying commercial."

Please!

Suddenly my computer *ding*ed. I had a new message on my facebook page from Friend! I guessed she was up and lonely like moi, hitting the info superhighway in search of like-minded pals.

Hey, sorry you feel down. I know, everything here can be really intense. But hang in there.

That was so nice! Wow.

Hey, thanks. I know. I just did something stupid, and I feel weird about it. I wish I could take it back, but I don't think I can. It's too hard to explain. . . .

Was it a bad idea to allude to the charm bracelet? No, I was being cryptic. I shouldn't worry. What if it was one of the Diamonds writing me? But I seriously doubted that. I quickly got a response.

I'm sure it's not that big of a deal . . . don't lose sleep over it. Speaking of which, time to turn in.

As long as I don't profit from it. That was it! I would tell Sofia I couldn't take the money from the heist. She could have it. A silly prank would not get anyone expelled.

Thanks, Friend, for the sage advice. Will you ever reveal yourself to me?

I sent along the message and waited.

In due time, Lucy. But for now, just know you have a friend.

I went back to bed and slept like a rock.

Chapter Fourteen

That Saturday after hoofing it on the court in scrambles matches, I almost fainted. We had been paired with various teammates round-robin style, and while I was very focused on my games, I could sense there was a buzz in the air. Victoria was absent, and Angelina was her usual sweet but reserved self, but a few of the girls on the doubles teams—who were practicing with us today—were whispering, and I picked up some chatter about Victoria. Maybe she was really sick? I tuned it out and headed back to the dorms.

* * *

"I have your cut. The Victoria von Hapsburg piece was a smash."

"Ah! You scared me, Sofia!" I said, closing my door quickly behind me. I was still dripping sweat from the morning's tennis practice—always way intense on Saturdays—and had rushed back to my room to shower rather than have to deal with perfect Angelina in the locker room. I had not expected to find Sofia sitting in the corner chair next to my window.

"Sorry, love, just thought you might want the money for the article, and I didn't want to leave it out."

So that's what they must have been murmuring about . . . Victoria's bracelet in the magazine.

"Um, yeah, about that," I said, opening my closet and putting my racket in the corner. "I don't want to take any money for this."

"Oh bollocks!" she said, flipping her hair confidently. "You have to. They were absolutely thrilled with the pics, and it's only fair that you get something for helping me. Four hundred thousand people read *Gab!* and, thanks to you, on page sixteen they will learn all about the lovely charm bracelet worn by a certain snot-nosed brat. It's all about young aristocracy these days. Readers can't get enough!"

I didn't like that Sofia was making it seem like I had cohatched the plan. I mean, I had helped her, but I never wanted to be accused of being such a deep conspirator. "Um, you know that it wasn't because of me. I just helped you out."

"Right, whateva," said Sofia dismissively.

"So, do you know what you're going to wear tonight?" I asked Sofia, changing the topic.

"Dad sent over a dress. Versace. He told his publisher that I absolutely had to play the part at the formals, so I get any designer gown I please."

"Wow, that's cool."

"Yeah, I can get you one if you want."

"No, that's okay. . . . "

Sofia stood up and walked over to me. She looked carefully in my eyes. "Don't freak out, Luce." She put her hands on my shoulders to comfort me. "It was just a silly prank."

"Right. Just a silly prank."

"Come on, why don't you take a bath and I'll wait for you in my room."

After a long, hot soak in the tub, and extra time lounging in my complimentary fluffy Frette bathrobe, I finally got dressed. As I gazed in my closet, I realized that Victoria was right—I had nothing to wear to Jazzmatazz. There was one dress that might pass muster—a dark blue, sleeveless minidress that had been my sister's—but I wasn't sure. I decided to bring it over to Sofia's room to see what she thought.

When I walked out in the hall holding the dress I heard a squeal of laughter and spun around.

"Nice dress!" said Iman with a wicked smirk.

"Oh my God, is *that* what you're wearing?" Antigone said with a laugh, literally covering her mouth in astonishment.

"What's wrong with it?" I asked. It was plain, but who cares?

"You really want to know?" asked Iman.

"In a word?" said Antigone, sizing it up and down. "Garish."

"How can it be garish? It's just a simple blue dress," I said, blood rushing to my head.

"Are you returning it to Sofia?" asked Iman snidely. "Or is it yours?"

"It's mine."

"You should stick to tennis whites, Sharapova," said Tiggy in the bitchiest tone ever. "Fashion is not your strong suit."

They exchanged amused looks before taking off down the hall. When they rounded the corner I heard them burst out laughing.

My blood was boiling when I entered Sofia's room. I held up the dress.

"Is this horrible? Some kind of fashion acne?" I demanded.

Sofia looked at it carefully. "It's not wonderful, but it's perfectly harmless."

"Iman and Antigone just made it seem like it was as bad as Britney Spears shaving her head."

Sofia rolled her eyes. "Those girls are just god-awful and nasty. Do you see why I have no qualms about playing pranks on them? They're spoiled little brats."

I was furious. "You're right. They are brats."

Sofia looked at me. "So let's get our revenge."

Chapter Fifteen

I wore the blue dress anyway. And guess what? It was so dark at the ball, you could barely see anyone's outfit. Jazzmatazz took place in the Crystal Cabaret Room, a leveled mini auditorium complete with supper-club tables, candlelit chandeliers, and even a cocktail waitress holding flapper-style 1920s cigarette boxes filled with (sugar-free) candy. The theme had been planned by the Decorating Committee, which essentially was made up of the senior and junior It girls plus, of course, the Diamonds. But their definition of decorating didn't mean staple guns and tinsel like in some American high school. It meant they *brought in* their own decorators, event specialists who were used to throwing royal weddings and charity balls throughout the Continent. For this particular escapade, Iman had wrangled the decorator from *Queer Eye*, who had just finished her older sister's deb ball in Paris.

"Isn't it simply divine?" Sofia gushed as we entered the transformed space. The tablecloths were made of raw quilted silk, and each student had his or her name and table number done in perfect calligraphy at the escort table by the grand flower-covered arched entryway. Sofia and I selected our cards.

"Seven," I read, praying hers was the same.

"Bollocks! I'm twenty-one. They clearly wanted to split us up. Iman is on the Events Committee. Bitch."

I got a shiver trying to imagine an interminable dinner with people I didn't even know. But then again, the bright side—maybe this would be a chance to meet someone new.

"Hey, lucky seven," I heard, turning to find Oliver standing over me. "We're at the same table." He smiled.

"Oh great!" I said, looking at Sofia, who shot me a wink. I wasn't quite sure what that signal meant.

"Can I get you ladies a drink?" Oliver offered.

"I'm okay, thanks. . . . " I demurred.

"You sure? They have killer mocktails, like Jimmy's Swisstini," he said.

"Jimmy is the eighty-seven-year-old bartender here," Sofia explained. "He's an institution."

"Wow, Oliver. I must say, that's what American guys would refer to as a chick drink," I teased.

"Well, we Brits have enough confidence in our virility to partake of so-called feminine beverages." He smiled. I blushed.

A tux-clad gentleman holding a baby handheld glockenspiel sounded the keys to announce dinner.

"I'm off to get a glass, then. See you in a moment at dinner." Oliver walked off, and I started to melt like the nearby giant ice sculpture of a trumpet.

"Oh my god. You were totally flirting with him!" Sofia accused.

"No I wasn't," I protested. *Was I?*

"Yes. You. Were," she said with her bony finger jutting at me. "Lucy. How are we supposed to get dirt on the royals if you're so up the royals' bums? You have to see it as predator and prey. Oliver wouldn't give a rat's arse about you if he knew your background, so don't melt at the sight of his batting lashes. Understood?"

"I guess."

"I'm only telling it like it is. Only true friends have candor like that."

"Okay."

"See you in the dessert lounge afterward." And with that Sofia turned and strode away to her table.

Alone in the midst of the crowd, I looked around, trying to find my social bearings. There were so many kids, luckily many of them now familiar from my seeing them in the dining room or teeing off at the golf range, which was by the courts.

"Hi, Lucy!" It was Rioko. "Thank you for your email—no worries!"

"Oh, I felt terrible about not getting it in time. I haven't been logging on at all."

"What table are you? I'm seven," she said, and suddenly in my head I heard happy violin music, knowing that I wouldn't be alone.

"Me too!" I exclaimed, genuinely happy. Rioko semed very friendly, and she had such a warm and sweet face that I always smiled when I saw her. We walked over to our table together.

Lucky table seven was covered in flowers—an explosion of three dozen peonies, with one more on each place setting, tied with a brown velvet ribbon. Crystal goblets glistened from the flickering light of fifty votives. Rioko was two down from me, and because it was boy-girl-boy-girl, I looked to see who was next to me. One place card bore Maxwell's name. Gag. On the other side there was a name I didn't know. Above my place card was a hand-calligraphied menu card with gilded edges listing the courses they would serve during the meal. I had never seen anything like it.

"Hi there, I'm Antony," said a chipper blond guy who approached the table, pulling out the chair beside me. "I see I'm your dinner partner."

"I'm Lucy."

"The tennis star, I know! Pleasure to make your acquaintance."

We shook hands just as Oliver came to the table holding two Swisstinis, one for him and the other for Angelina, who was, of course, seated beside him.

"Let's get this paaartay started!" screamed Maxwell, who sidled up to the table like he owned it. "Hey, ladies, lookin' sharp!" he said after scanning everyone. Which meant scanning their chests. Gross.

"Lucy, Lucy, Luuucy," Maxwell said, looking me over. I suddenly felt like a rotisserie chicken turning under the gaze of his lecherous eyes on my boobs. "Smart dress."

I wanted to boil myself, I felt so grody, but instead I managed somehow to mutter a weak "Thanks."

Antony leaned in to whisper, "Lucy, don't mind that jerk, he's a bit of a clod." I smiled. Here I didn't even know this guy and he read my mind.

"I noticed. So where are you from, Antony?"

"I was born in London, but we moved around quite a bit. My parents are now in Australia, and I spent five years in your country, actually."

"Really? That's great, where?"

"Boston. My mum taught at Harvard, and then we left when I was in eighth grade and I came here. I'm a junior. I really miss the States. Such a freedom to it, less snobbish," he whispered, leaning in.

It was true. Sure, there were snobs everywhere, but the whole emphasis on who came from where was clearly a European thing.

No one spoke much of lineage when we visited the U.S. I think my cousins in Chicago didn't even know what the word meant.

Antony and I chatted for what seemed like an hour, eating our blini and frisée salads with truffle oil. Until Maxwell had to go and shake things up.

"Antony, why're you hogging Lucy? It's my turn, bloke."

And with that Maxwell put his arm around me. I shuddered and for some reason looked across the table at Oliver, who had been talking closely with Angelina. She looked absolutely breathtaking in a beaded floor-length silver gown. He glanced up at the same time and our eyes met. He was larger than life with his confident warmth and the way he always made me feel like I was the only person in the room. But, like they say about Bill Clinton, he probably had that sincere connection with everyone he focused his laser beam on. Angelina was certainly blessed to be the girl he chose to spend time with.

"Okay, Lucy. Tell me your deepest, darkest fantasies," Maxwell said, staring into my eyes. I leaned away from him. He leaned closer and stroked my shoulder with his grimy paw. I pulled back, visibly repulsed.

"Buddy, lay off," commanded Oliver from across the table. Drama!

"C'mon, man, you get all the tail you want. I'm just making a move here on Van Pelt's own little Sharapova!"

"She's not *tail*," corrected Antony, standing up.

"Whoa, whoa, whoa, chill out, man. Who're you, friggin' Lancelot now? Sheesh," Maxwell taunted.

Rather than engage, Antony came to the rescue and reached out his hand. "Lucy, would you care to dance?"

Gladly. I practically leaped up and followed Antony to the dance floor, where he expertly put his arm around me. I tried to match his perfect moves as Mr. Marsalis's music filled the air.

"Listen, Lucy, those guys—the whole lot of them—are spoiled rich arses. You just have to tune them out." I looked over his shoulder at our table—Rioko now on the receiving end of Maxwell's advances—and saw Oliver watching us.

"Oliver seems nice though," I offered.

"Don't be deceived. We were friends last year, but he's not so great. Better to just steer clear."

His take on Oliver didn't seem possible. He was so charming! Maybe that was it—could I have been sucked in by his warm smiles and royal polish? Hmm. I guess it was possible that even my animal instincts were flawed sometimes, especially in this lion's den.

"And that bloke Maxwell, what a rude, raving idiot," he said, shaking his head.

"Yeah, he's the worst," I agreed. "What's his problem, anyway?"

"He's the black sheep of his family dynasty. His great-great-grandfather invented the first golf carts and they produce almost every one in the world. It's a monopoly, really. Anyway, his brothers are all quite successful, nice chaps, but Max has a bunch of problems, including that he slept with a married woman whose husband is the head of the bank his family works with. Miles Bristol."

"No way! How old is she?"

"Like, thirty-two. Talk about *Desperate Housewives*. Anyway, it was all shushed up. But as you just had the unfortunate experience of seeing for yourself, that guy can only think with his down-yonders."

Fascinating.

Chapter Sixteen

I could hardly contain myself when I got to the bathroom with Sofia, who had gestured to me after my dance with Antony. She locked the door behind me.

"Antony is so cute! Are you having fun?" she gushed.

"Antony is great!" I said. "And I got major Maxwell gossip, too!

"*That's* my girl!" beamed Sofia, eyes ablaze. "Out with it!"

I told her what Antony had said.

"Who was the woman married to?" she demanded, on fire with curiosity.

"Oh, I don't know, I've never heard of him. Miles somebody. In banking."

"Wait, Miles *Bristol*? As in the richest man who's not in oil? *Holy moly!* This is a page-four story, Luce! This is ten grand for us! I'm calling Daddy—"

"No, Sofia, don't—" As much as I couldn't stand Maxwell, I hadn't meant for this news to end up in the pages of *Gab!* magazine.

"Don't worry, don't worry," she cooed, glancing in the mirror to freshen her lip gloss. "You did great. Now we can hit Club Platinum for the after party and not even worry about the tab. 'Cause I got way more cashola coming in after this killer tidbit. Thanks, love." Sofia puckered up her newly glossed lips and walked out. I followed her, stressed to the core.

Back at the tables, people had finished their main courses and were proceeding to the dessert lounge, a swanky sweets buffet with couches and coffee tables upholstered in red velvet against the starry black and silver background. There was a jazz quartet playing in the corner, and I felt like I had been transported back in time to some Harlem club. Even with all my internal turmoil about Sofia's loose-lipped plans, this was truly the most exquisite evening I'd ever had. I dipped strawberries into the rich chocolate fondue fountain, which cascaded with rippling sweet-smelling chocolate. After about ten I thought I'd pass out.

"Brilliant, right?" Oliver was beside me, dipping a stick of buttery pound cake into the velvety chocolate.

"Yes, I'm literally high right now. This is beyond incredible," I gushed. "I'm having the best time."

"Are you?" Oliver asked.

"Yes, this is unlike any other party I've ever been to!"

"Listen, Lucy," he said, putting his hand on my shoulder. I would be lying if I didn't admit I felt tingling where his hand was. As he moved me off to the side, I spotted Antony with his back to us ordering more ginger ales. "About Antony—," Oliver started.

"What is it?" I asked, turning my attention back to him and noticing the furrow in Oliver's brow.

"Just be . . . careful." What the hell did that mean?

"He's a nice guy, Oliver. I'm not worried. Anyway, nothing's going on—we just met tonight."

"All right, then, I just—" He paused, holding my wrist lightly in his hand. I almost fainted.

Just then Antony walked up. Speak of the devil.

"What, warning her about me?" said Antony with a sly smile.

"No, no, I just— Have a lovely night," said Oliver, and he left us. I saw Angelina waiting for him and he led her outside, where the cars were waiting to take everyone to the after party at Club Platinum.

"So, are we going or are we going?" Sofia squealed, running over. "The night is but a fetus."

Chapter Seventeen

*C*lub Platinum had dark banquettes all around the perimeter of the cool, dimly lit space. It was clearly the It place for people to mingle, and I saw many of my classmates, including Iman, Antigone, and Victoria, hug the bouncer upon entry, then warmly greet the maître d' with a kiss on the cheek. Lola and Rocky, prominent DJs on the Euro club circuit, were spinning in the raised corner booth. Sofia was clearly soaking it all up as she described how "major" the scene was that night.

"I mean, Lola and Rocky won't play one record without a

hundred thousand euros. They're huge. They played the after party of the Duke of Faxington's daughter's wedding in Marbella. Oh! There's Holly Bollycock of the Bollycock Tea empire. . . . "

Her wide eyes drank in every sexy, preened teen in the joint, and Antony, who'd sat with us in a plum corner spot, laughed in amusement. "She's quite something, your friend," he murmured. "She's like a Who's Who compendium of the whole Continent."

"Try *world*," I corrected.

"Shall we have a go?" he said, gesturing to the packed dance floor where Antigone and Moabi LeTroux were practically Lambada-ing themselves into one being, and Iman and Morgan Wellington, the cricket star, were doing quasi-medical procedures on each other's tonsils. While thoroughly grossed out by their PDA, I must say, I was jealous that they'd found someone they liked. Following him out into the crowd, I wondered if maybe Antony might be the one to put a little spark in my semester.

As he twirled me around I saw Oliver walk in with Angelina. He looked at us, then looked away.

Then I glanced over at Sofia, who was holding up her drink. But next to the glass I saw a huge cocktail ring I hadn't noticed earlier. She sipped her drink and kept touching the big onyx ring with the other hand. In the whirling collage of thumping beats, glittering clothes, flailing dancing limbs, and blurred strobe lights, not a soul but me would ever notice. As I watched her carefully, I saw her touch the ring, adjusting it and moving her hand in different positions on the table. She kept lifting her hand for no reason, and tilting it at various angles. Suddenly, dancing to the music under the strobe lights, I realized that the onyx in that huge setting was hardly a simple piece of shiny black rock. It was the lens of a tiny camera that was quietly clicking away at the unknowing glamorous couples who shimmied and spun to the turntable music, beautiful heads thrown back in laughter, without a care in the world.

Five days later when the glossy issue of *GAB!* hit the newsstands, the school was wildly abuzz with the explosive ten-page feature on Van Pelt. Antigone and Moabi's hookup was now international news. Her whole country was practically planning the wedding for their new queen-to-be and her prince, Moabi.

Ditto for Iman, whose strict father sent emissaries to bring her home for the following weekend for fear the cricket jock would deflower his only daughter. There were even rumors that he was also humiliated by the makeout photos because he'd promised her hand to a diamond magnate family in Nigeria. Tongues wagged. Sofia beamed.

I knew exactly what was going on but never brought up the camera I'd noticed on Sofia's finger. That was until I read the "Hot Goss" blurb that described, verbatim, Maxwell's dalliances with Mrs. Bristol. After the party the other night I'd finally gotten her to promise that she wouldn't say anything about that piece of gossip.

"Sofia!" I snapped, throwing the magazine down on her bed.

"It's one thing to take photos at Club Platinum—that's your issue. But to print that Maxwell stuff? I mean, that woman is married!"

"So? They did it—it's their problem."

"But Antony told me that stuff! Now he'll hate me."

"No he won't," she said. "Trust me. He won't."

"How do you know?" I asked, still embarrassed by my big mouth.

"He doesn't read *Gab!* Take it from me. Don't stress. Listen, when people have affairs, it gets out there! It's not as if he'd be the only person who knew! Plus, hello, Lucy—he'd never in a million years put two and two together. Calm down."

I stormed back to my room. I suddenly felt really dirty and ashamed of even knowing about Sofia's capers. I went online and found a message from Friend that read:

Hi there, Lucy. Did you have fun at Jazzmatazz? You seemed to be enjoying yourself on that dance floor ☺ Into that guy?

A smile crept across my face, as I certainly would never talk to Sofia about such things. *The jury's out,* I typed. *How about you? Did you have fun?* I hit Send and looked out the window, feeling my heart race with nervous anxiety. When I didn't get an immediate response, I took to the only place where I could get out my aggression: the courts.

* * *

I think I hit the ball so hard I could hear little tiny screams coming from the fluorescent furry Wilson casing.

"Wow, that's some serve," I heard Oliver call. I turned to find him picking up a ball in the hopper—something only the assistants normally did.

"Hi, Oliver. What're you doing here?"

"Same as you, I suppose. Just wanted to keep going, you know, blow off steam."

"Yeah, well, you got me. I certainly have been stressed out lately," I vented.

"Course work? Or . . . other things?"

"Not so much the academics, thankfully. Just other stuff, I guess."

"Listen, I'm here if you ever want to talk. I know how it goes here. It's a bit of a hornet's nest, this school."

"Yeah, well, I just hope I don't get stung." I smiled. "But thanks, Oliver. I appreciate it."

"Well, Lucy, I'll leave you to your serve crunching, then." He patted me on the back, smiled sweetly, and went to the court next to me with his full ball hopper. We made our serves for another hour, occasionally glancing at each other, an unspoken easiness settling over us.

It would be nice to talk to someone about what was going on, but I felt strange opening up to Oliver, given his gentle attempt to warn me about Antony. I knew he was nice and was trying to be my friend, in a way, but why would he shoot down another guy? It was so out of the blue. It was clear Oliver was into Angelina, not me; they were always together. So what would be his problem with Antony? I had to get to the bottom of it, and fortunately the opportunity presented itself sooner than I thought.

Chapter Eighteen

A few days later, Antony called me for brunch, and I met him for a feast of chef-prepared *pain perdu* (aka French toast; *perdu* means "lost" in French, as in the bread gets lost in the egg, and subsequently my thighs). He was very flirtatious on the phone, and I remembered how much fun we had dancing at the club. Maybe this could turn into something. Still, my feelings for Antony were conflicted. He was a handsome guy, witty and charming, and had more social ease than most guys I knew his age. I was flattered that he seemed interested in me. Guys were never exactly beating down my door, and quite frankly his attention made me semiswoony. But okay, full disclosure: even though I knew the prince (i.e., Oliver) could get any princess he wanted, there was something about him that made my heart flutter. Watching him on the tennis court could make me faint, he was so graceful. He was nice to me when no one else on the team gave me the time of day. And he was, after all, a prince. I mean, weren't we all raised on Cinderella stories?

That said, Antony was still interesting to me. We ended up having a really nice time at brunch, and then he walked me down the path to my dorm.

"So how are you finding it here?" Antony asked as we approached the garden.

"I like it. It's, you know, different. I'm not really used to this kind of scene."

"I know, I know. I can imagine it would be very different from the places you grew up," said Antony.

"*That's* an understatement," I said, nodding.

"This place is probably pretty feeble," he said.

I smiled. I liked that he had a sense of humor. "Totally. I mean, the fact that they only have *one* maid per room? What kind of a school is this?"

Antony looked at me, at first surprised, but then he smiled. "Right. Never thought of that."

"I mean, what am I supposed to do when it's her break? Pick up my clothes myself?" I said, continuing to joke. The absurdity of this place was now hitting me.

"I know, right? I am the biggest slob. I need someone to look after me at all times!"

"And what's up with the heavy textbooks? Couldn't they find someone to carry them for us? And the sheets! They may say the thread count is four hundred, but it feels like *two hundred* to me."

"I'm astonished! Really?" said Antony, looking mock horrified.

I clucked my tongue dramatically. "Yup, there's no place like home, I tell you. No place like home."

"Well, your home must be pretty spectacular," he said, taking my hand. He rubbed his thumb against my palm and squeezed, sending shivers to the tips of my toes. We were in front of my dorm now, and I knew that there might be people in the lounge who would be witness to this, but I didn't care.

"It is," I almost whispered, caught up by the intense look in his eyes.

"I'd love to see it sometime," he said softly, leaning in close. I felt woozy.

"Sure" was all I could squeak out.

"Well, bye now," he said gently, with a final hand squeeze.

"Bye," I said.

I watched him walk away down the path. He turned around once and waved, and I blushed, embarrassed that he knew I was watching him go. It was so surreal for me to have this cute guy in a tweed blazer and gray flannels, the picture of elegance, be into me. I couldn't believe my luck.

Chapter Nineteen

"So are you with Antony now?" asked Iman, her arms folded in a huff and her eyebrows raised. I knew I had felt someone's eyes on me through the curtains.

"No, um, I mean, we're friends."

"First you go for Oliver, and now his arch nemesis? You really try to get around," she said snidely.

What was she implying? So many girls and guys here were hooking up, why was *I* being singled out for "getting around"? Pathetic.

"That's so not the case, but whatever. And what's your problem, anyway?" I asked, feeling quite brave.

Iman seemed genuinely shocked that I dared question her. "No problem," she said evenly. "Just noticing."

I was dying to ask her about the background of Oliver and Antony being enemies, but I didn't want to engage her with any more conversation. Instead I stomped up the steps toward Sofia's room and knocked on the door.

"Come in," she called.

"I'm *fed up* with those Diamonds! They know how to ruin every good moment!" I practically yelled as I slammed the door. Sofia's mouth curled into a smile.

"What've they done now, love?"

"Iman is implying I'm a slut. She says I am flirting with Oliver and Antony, which is a total lie!"

"Why, are you into Oliver? Or Antony? Or both?"

"No! How could I be? Oliver's a friggin' prince, and he's totally unavailable—it's not like I'd ever go for him. And Antony—I'm not sure yet. But why do they even care?"

"Because they're bored, sad girls who have nothing better to do. I told you, they're awful!"

"Meanwhile," I probed, "do you know anything about Oliver and Antony? Some kind of falling-out?"

She whipped around. "No. What is it?"

I immediately regretted that I'd said anything. Now I never knew when I was talking to Sofia as a friend or as a spy for *Gab!*

"I don't know," I said lamely. "Iman said something about it."

"Interesting," said Sofia, eyes sparkling. "I'll have to get to the bottom of that."

"Please don't, Sofia," I begged. "Let this one go. I feel pretty nauseous about all this stuff now."

Sofia smiled. "Don't. Look, I know you are conflicted, but, well, I didn't want to say anything . . . "

"What?"

"The Diamonds are somehow under the impression that you're like this major slut. There's even a rumor that you, um, you know, with Oliver."

The blood drained from my face. "What?" I gasped.

"Look, I told them it's a lie, right away. And I think they knew that. But the point is, for some reason they think you're a threat, and they are going to spread rumors about you. So maybe it's time we do the same for them."

I thought for a minute. "Like what?"

"Nothing weird. I mean, you know how Tiggy passed out in the hall after Jazzmatazz?"

"She did?!"

"Yes, I thought everyone knew that. Now next time we just need a picture. That will say it all."

"I don't know . . . "

"Look, you have to discredit these people. Once they have no credibility, no one will believe their lies about you."

I lay back on her mass of pillows and pondered.

"Come on! We just need to catch them doing something mean or bad. Give them a dose of their own medicine. Catch them in a lie, or hurting someone. You know they made Rioko cry?"

"They did?"

"Yeah. They were pissed at her for practicing early one morning and interrupting their 'beauty sleep' so they took her violin and threw it to one another, almost breaking it! That thing is worth, like, a million bucks."

"Oh my gosh, that's so evil. She is the sweetest—"

"That's what they are! *Evil*," said Sofia, flipping her hair back and straightening the pleats in her skirt. "That's why we have to stick up for the little people!"

"We'll see. If the opportunity arises . . . "

"Great!"

The opportunity arose faster than I thought it would.

Chapter Twenty

I awoke to the sound of a little *ping* from my computer, which I'd left on by accident. Thank goodness. I wearily rose to see what had arrived in my in-box. It was from Friend.

> Lucy—I hate to be the loathed messenger, but I wanted to tell you that Iman & her gang are doing something to your door. . . .

I jumped up and opened it abruptly, hearing titters of laughter and running footsteps down the hall. No one was to be seen. I looked at my door, which was covered in a collage of all kinds of *Playboy* centerfolds with my face taped on the heads. I was astonished. One was even nude with a tennis racket. Jesus. I started ripping them down piece by grody piece. When every last tape remnant had been peeled, I smashed it all into the trash and took to my computer.

Thanks, Friend. These girls are such raging beeyotches to me and I have no idea what I've ever done. Ugh . . . did you see them doing the deed?

I hit Send.
A few minutes later, the reply:

I have my eyes in many places. ☺ I just want to look out for you . . . they're pretty terrible.

Hmm . . . maybe it was Rioko? I knew she was on a par with me in loathing those snobbish freaks. I couldn't be sure, but this time I was *really* mad. My parents always joke that I am so easy and laid-back unless you cross me and then I have a huge temper. It takes a lot to provoke me, but once there, I really go nuts. And I had reached the boiling point. I was so sick of the petty tricks these spoiled girls were doing. Enough already!

I knocked on Sofia's door.

"So, ready to rumble?" she said, framed by the carved mahogany.

"Abso-friggin'-lutely."

* * *

Cue the *Mission: Impossible* music. With eyes darting in either direction, Sofia took my hand and led me into her room, closing the door behind us. There was a metal trunk at the foot of her bed. She expertly opened it, and I was stunned to see a Quantico-level amalgam of wires, plugs, and small boxes inside.

"Um, is that a bomb?" I asked naively.

"Hello? I'm an aspiring journalist, not a terrorist!" she replied, incredulous. I wasn't quite sure how she was a *journalist* per se, but whatever. "These are state-of-the-art bugging devices. Daddy just had them shipped. These tiny fiber optics will watch and hear their every move."

She started nimbly connecting wires and cables together like she'd done it a million times before. I stood motionless, brow furrowed, once again oscillating between my full-body loathing of Iman, Antigone, and Victoria and the diametrically opposed yearning to be above them and just brush it off. But the vision of my head on the greased-up tanorexic bods on my door continued to make my blood boil.

"I can't do this without you, Wimbledon," she said, reading my ambivalence. "You in?"

"I'm in," I replied shakily.

"Good," she said, a smile spreading as a twinkle glistened in her mischievous eye. "The Diamonds are about to get seriously flawed."

107

Chapter Twenty-One

That night, while the gals hit Club Platinum, Sofia and I snuck down the hall. I kept watch while she darted mouselike into each of the three witches' rooms, wiring away as I stood nervously by, the sound of my breath making me all the more neurotic. Suddenly I heard steps coming in the direction of the wing I was standing in.

"Sofia," I whispered. "Someone's coming!"

I guess she hadn't heard me because she didn't exit. I panicked. Who would be there when everyone was out? I drew a sharp breath when I saw who it was—the elusive and stunning Angelina. She looked at me and gave a tight half smile and slight nod in acknowledgment of my existence.

"Hi, Lucy," she said quietly.

"Hey . . . " was my feeble semiresponse.

"What are you up to?"

"Up to? Um . . . nothing, just . . . waiting for someone. You?"

"I'm tired. I was going to go to bed."

"No Platinum?" I asked, wondering why she wasn't dancing on tables like everyone else who was fabulous.

"Nope. That scene's not really for me. It's fun and all, I suppose—I'm just . . . more of a homebody, I guess."

"I hear you. Me too." It was refreshing that she wasn't partying her panties off like every other illustrious and beautiful teen on the Continent.

She was about to go, but then she hesitated. "If you're just hanging out, do you want to come in and watch *The Hills*? It's supposed to be a crazy episode—the girls get into some catfight. Kind of like here."

That was all I wanted to do right now! But instead I was stuck being Sofia's accomplice. "Oh my gosh, that's so nice, Angelina, but I'm kind of waiting for Sofia. I promised her I would—"

She cut me off. "It's okay, next time," she said, smiling.

"Definitely!" I said, with a little too much enthusiasm.

"Okay, well, I'm off to bed," she said shyly. "Good night."

"Good night!"

I was thrilled that she left before realizing what Sofia and I were up to but bummed that I had to rebuff her first overture at friendship. I bet the Diamonds would go insane to know she'd asked me to hang with her! That was almost better revenge than wiring their rooms. But for now I was just glad she didn't catch us. As she walked down the hall, I exhaled in relief but was still shifting from side to side like a child who has to pee until Sofia exited the final room.

"What took you so long?" I demanded. "I almost had a heart attack! Angelina came by and could have busted us!"

"Cool your jets, Wimbledon! The wheels are in motion."

"Yeah, and if we ever get caught she'll know it's me!"

"Chill out, dahhhling. Stress is not becoming." Sofia breezed by me, back down the hall to her room.

"So what now?" I asked as she casually pulled a disco dress from her closet, acting as if she'd just brushed her teeth or checked her email rather than planted spy devices.

"We're hitting Club Plat like everyone else! There's nothing else to do except party—the action will all go down after curfew, when they come home to dissect the evening! Till then, let's rage."

I reluctantly went back to my room to get changed and found my phone ringing.

"Lucy, where are you? Everyone's out!" It was Antony. Maybe going out wasn't such a bad idea.

"Oh, um, hi—I'm . . . on my way."

"Can't wait to see you."

As I hung up I got a jolt of excitement—tonight was finally going to be the night that Miss Tennis Racket also felt like a pretty girl at the dance, now that a perfectly charming boy was into her. And it felt great.

Antony was waiting for us with a perfect corner booth when Sofia and I arrived. The three of us hung out, Sofia wearing her big cocktail ring again. Antony asked me to dance, and when we were on the floor twirling and laughing, I noticed two security guards with wires in their ears step into the club. They looked straight out of an espionage movie. I couldn't figure out what they were doing there. I mean, everyone there was security-worthy, but once we were on the grounds of campus and in the town, students were pretty much safe. But then I gulped. What if they were on the hunt for us? Paranoid, I signaled to Sofia, thinking they might be on the prowl for the person who took all those photos for *Gab!* She nodded, acknowledging my heads-up, and discreetly put her hand under the table. No use risking it. Not that they would realize that her ring was a camera, but hey, you never know.

Just then Victoria and Iman walked by me (Antigone was nearby on the dance floor, she and Moabi LeTroux making out again like minks on a breeding farm) and literally did the Slut Sneeze to me. As in fifth grade. As in *aaaaahhhh-choo* form but by saying "Slut." I looked at Antony, morbidly embarrassed. Trying to recover, I shook my head and rolled my eyes.

"Those girls have it in for me."

I tried to shake off their juvenile behavior, but he wouldn't have it. He stormed up behind them and tapped Victoria on the shoulder. "Lame, Tory."

"Oh chill out, we're just having fun," she sneered. "Tell her to thicken her skin."

"You're a sad, pathetic girl. Back. Off. Her. *Now!*"

Wow, chivalry! I must say, they looked frightened. They slowly walked away but not before shooting me an acidic look of death.

"Thanks, Antony. . . . "

"Let's get out of here," he said indignantly.

I went to go tell Sofia we were leaving.

"Oh, I'm off, too. I'm gonna get the headphones on for a looong night of Lucy bashing on the wires!" she said.

Great.

I walked outside, heart heavy, to find Antony waiting for me in the moonlight as the party raged on inside the club.

"Why the glum look? Don't tell me you really care about what those sad girls think?"

"Those sad girls are about to rip me to shreds," I muttered. "I never did a thing to them!"

"Listen, my dear girl, they're simply jealous of you."

"Jealous? Of *me*? Antony, you're—"

"I'm right," he said, taking my hand. "You have it all: brains, beauty, talent, a good family. . . . "

How did he know about my family? We hadn't spoken much about my parents.

" . . . and a guy who's crazy about you."

Really? *Moi?* I blushed to a happy peony pink.

At that sudden moment, the mean girls, the tests, the upcoming tennis match, the spy capers with Sofia—none of it mattered. And as Antony leaned in slowly and kissed me, taking me in his arms, I didn't mind if he was the only soul in Europe who cared about me. In his embrace, one was enough.

Chapter Twenty-Two

I was nervous. I mean, sweating bullets. It was our first tennis match, and we were playing a school that was also known to have a fantastic tennis team. It was just a "scramble," meaning that it was supposed to be for fun and not count, since the real tennis season didn't start until the spring, but I had been told that in truth everything counts. In fact, Coach Sachs had made it clear that our days and nights would be brutal if we didn't nail this one. I had called my parents the night before in a panic.

"Sweetheart, you're a wonderful tennis player. I'm sure you

will do great," said my ever-supportive mother.

"But, Mom, you're used to me playing against people who don't really matter. This is major. We're playing a team that has a former Olympic coach leading them."

"Don't worry, it will be fine."

My dad was no better but in a different way. "Go get 'em tiger—you know you need to win to get a good tennis scholarship for college," he commanded. He always had tennis scholarship on the brain. Sometimes I wish he would back off a little. But when I thought of my sister and her only option being an ROTC scholarship, I knew deep down he was right. I wanted to go to a good college, and tennis was the ticket.

Thankfully the game was to be on our home turf. I didn't want to deal with traveling somewhere, and this team was flying in from Les Abeilles in the Loire Valley. I got to the courts early, determined to stretch and be fully limber by the time practice started. It was still dark when I got to the locker rooms to change, and the sun was just rising when I made it out to the court. I shivered a little in the cold and was a bit dismayed to see how my breath hung in the air, but I knew as soon as I did some laps I'd warm right up.

"Hey," said a voice behind me.

I turned around, startled.

"Hi, Oliver."

"Couldn't sleep either?"

"Nope," I said, placing my rackets on the bench and stretching my arms out to keep warm. "I'm kind of a nervous wreck!"

"Me too," Oliver admitted. He smiled and shook his head. "My bloody nerves get me every time."

I loved that Oliver always seemed to tell the truth. You'd think that he would be more rigid, being a prince and all. It was very refreshing. Since kissing Antony on Saturday night, I'd fully had Antony on the brain. I was always the type who liked the guys who liked me—not some delusional chaser of the It boy. And seeing Oliver now, I realized that since he would never be a possibility, and didn't need to be, it would be really nice to have him as a friend. So what if it caused problems with Angelina and the Diamonds? That was actually more *their* problem than mine.

"Wanna do some laps?" I asked. Then, not knowing what seized me, I sprinted ahead. "Race you!"

"Hey, no fair!" said Oliver, tearing off his sweatshirt and taking off after me.

We did several fast loops around the court, teasingly passing each other now and then. We ultimately slid into a steady jogging pace, determined not to overdo it before the game. It was fun running with someone else. We didn't say anything, really, just smiled at each other every once in a while.

As we rounded the court for something like our sixteenth lap, a loud giggling shriek pierced the air. I saw Chérie, the buxom blonde who worked in the school store, walking out of the flower-covered gazebo with her head thrown back in laughter. Everyone knew Chérie. She was in her early twenties, and the rumor was that she was "available for a good time" for any young man at school who had a sizeable bank account. Which was every guy in school. Supposedly a lot of boys had lost their virginity to her. I thought it was odd that she was up and about so early, but I kept up my pace. When I rounded the court again I could have sworn I also saw Antony walking by the same gazebo that Chérie came out of. I waved as I jogged on, but then suddenly realized that what I just witnessed was even more strange. Was that really Antony? What was he doing there? And was he with Chérie? I had gone by so quickly that I didn't see if he waved back, but I didn't want to stop now and have Oliver think something was up. I kept running, faster now, but when I came around to the corner where I had seen them both, no one was there. Was I hallucinating? The boy I had spotted was wearing the same peacoat that Antony always wore, had the same brown hair—although a lot of kids at school had the same coat.

"I gotta take a break," I said, stopping when we got to the bench. I bent over, hands on hips, and took deep breaths. Had Antony been hooking up with Chérie? Was I paranoid?

"Well done, Lucy. You should consider track," said Oliver.

"Yeah," I mumbled before I took a large swig out of my water bottle. "Hey, you didn't happen to see who was out in the gazebo, did you?" I asked, pretending to be nonchalant.

"Oh, er," began Oliver. "I think I saw Chérie."

"Did you see who she was with?" I asked, emboldened some-how. I did not want to be made a fool of. If Antony was getting down with Chérie, I wanted to know.

Oliver looked at me carefully. "Listen, Lucy, I wanted to talk to you about Antony."

"What do you mean?" I asked. Could he read my mind? Or had he seen what I did?

"He's . . . he's tricky. He has one thing in mind, and—this will come out the wrong way—you are not his usual type of girl, which makes me worry. For you. I just don't feel that he has the right intentions," Oliver said with a sigh.

I was speechless. Should I feel good that Oliver was protecting me? Or was there something else? I was about to speak when we were interrupted by none other than Antony himself.

"There you are! I was just coming up to wish you good luck," said Antony, giving me a big hug. I stared at Oliver over Antony's shoulder. He looked away and excused himself, mumbling something about practicing serves, and left us alone.

"Antony, did I just see you with Chérie?" I asked flatly.

"You *did*! That old cow! She was leaving Rolf's room and lost her shoe along the path. I was helping her find it. I told her she'd better learn to keep her clothes on."

Relief swept through my body. Antony hadn't even paused or seemed remotely disconcerted when I brought up Chérie, the Van Pelt school bicycle (everyone's had a ride). Either he was an Academy Award–winning actor or he was telling the truth.

"Oh, because, you know, I wanted to make sure it wasn't *you* and Chérie in that romantic gazebo," I said, looking him in the eye. "Sofia told me that's where people go to fool around."

"Look at you!" said Antony, his eyes crinkling with laughter. "I didn't fancy you to be the jealous type! But no, I can assure you I would never go for that skank. She's been around the block more times than the ex–Mrs. Federline. Dirty."

Okay, fair enough. I felt somewhat relieved.

"So, Luce, what were you doing with Mr. Majesty? That bloke is such a wanker."

I stiffened, feeling weirdly defensive of Oliver. Antony obviously read my reaction and reached for me.

"Come here," he said, taking my sweaty arm and steering me to the side of the court. I decided to take the plunge.

"Antony, what's the deal with you and Oliver?" I asked. I mean, elephant in the room.

Antony sighed and looked up at the sky. "I can honestly say I don't know!"

I gave him a quizzical look and he continued. "Okay, there was this time when I was going after this girl—I think she's, like, his cousin or something, in that poshy London scene he runs around with. Anyway, he totally talked her out of me. I think honestly that he is just a huge snob. My parents are not as wealthy as his are and I think he has a problem with it."

"That doesn't sound like Oliver."

"How well do you know him?" asked Antony, cocking his head to the side.

"I don't know, he just doesn't seem like a snob."

"Did you know he got in huge trouble last year for yelling some nasty comment at another bloke at a football—er, soccer to you—game? Started a whole riot."

"That can't be true. . . . "

"It is. Check it out," he said, nodding vehemently. "You'd be surprised by the prince. He isn't all that regal."

I glanced over at Oliver, who was practicing his perfect ace of a serve. He just didn't strike me as the type to do something like that.

"He's always nice to me," I said feebly.

"And why wouldn't he be, my dear! You have it all—looks, brains, class, money . . . "

I laughed at the last part. "Oh yeah, big money."

"I love your audacity!" said Antony with a laugh, putting his arms around me and leaning in.

We managed to steal a quick kiss before Coach Sachs and the rest of the team arrived and it was time for real practice. Antony reluctantly waved and left for his rugby practice, but he promised to come back and watch when it was my turn to play.

Invigorated by his being in the stands, I managed to whip my opponent's butt, 6–love, 6–love. Only, when I looked up in the stands and saw Antony pumping his fist in the air with every point I scored, I felt like I was the one getting the love.

Chapter Twenty-Three

"There is something about that here," said Sofia, pulling out an old issue of *Gab!* from the storage boxes under her bed.

She handed me an article from the previous year that was titled "Spoiled Prince Disses Common Man." I couldn't believe my eyes. The article told how Oliver had caused a *major* meltdown at a Chelsea–Tottenham soccer game. I was shocked. I couldn't believe it was my Oliver—I mean, um, Oliver Oliver. So weird. But sure enough, there was a picture of him, looking angry and being restrained by cops. Wow. I guess you never know people.

"Funny, right?" asked Sofia, staring at me.

"Yeah, I can't quite put that together with him. He seems so sweet."

"He is divine-looking. So tell me about Antony. Now *he* is hot!"

I spent the next half hour filling her in on all the nitty-gritty of my burgeoning relationship. We were seated on her fluffy rug, the fire was going, and as she asked question after question, I was all too eager to tell her every little detail, every innermost thought.

"That's fabulous," she said when I was finally done.

"So what about you? Is there anyone you like?" I asked, feeling bad that I had been such a conversation hog.

"I have my eye on someone," she said, smiling. "But it's too early to tell. I'll let you know."

"Okay," I said, suddenly wishing that I had not downloaded every gory deet to her when she was being as closemouthed as a president under investigation. I had that sensation you get when you eat too much Chinese food or popcorn, which is great while you do it, but afterward you want to vomit. Had I revealed too much?

"What I do want to discuss is how awesomely our little project worked! Come here," she said, leading me over to her computer.

She sat down and clicked through several files, and suddenly Victoria, Iman, and Antigone's rooms all came on the screen. I was shocked. Victoria wasn't in there, but Iman was sitting on her bed chatting on the phone, and Antigone was doing yoga on a mat. I was riveted.

"Oh my God!"

"I know," said Sofia, beaming proudly. "Okay, this is just boring stuff. Let me show you what I got from a few days ago."

Sofia scanned through her files and clicked on one called "Extremely Entertaining."

"I've already had fun doing some editing. You're going to die! Here, sit down."

I slid into Sofia's seat while she stood and leaned over me from behind. I watched as the screen changed to show Antigone's room. There she was, totally naked, and, um, having a go with Moabi. I couldn't believe what I was seeing. It was pretty graphic. I could tell Sofia was watching my face, and when things got a little too heavy, I had to look away.

"Brilliant, right?"

"Sofia, we can't do anything with this. It's total invasion of privacy," I said, suddenly panicky. What had we done? This was major.

"Of course we can! They're evil. We can do whatever we want."

"But, Sofia, this will totally ruin her reputation. Her parents will kill her, we could get thrown out, it's so so bad. . . . "

Sofia furrowed her brows. "No, we can! No one will know it's us. And besides, it will probably be the best thing that ever happened to her. Look at Paris Hilton! She was nothing until her sex tape."

"But the difference is that Paris *knew* that guy was taping her, and everyone suspects she even leaked the tape. Antigone had no idea. No, we can't do anything."

"Yes we can, and we will," said Sofia, crossing her arms defiantly.

It became a staredown.

"Sofia, you know this is not right," I said gently, trying another tactic.

"Why is it not right? It is, after all, against school rules to have boys in our rooms, never mind doing what Antigone was doing!"

"But we were spying on her!"

"So what? It's her fault," said Sofia. "Listen, Lucy. These girls are nasty tarts. I don't know why in the world you would stick up for them. They are evil, evil, rich snotty wankers and we have to get back at them. We have to ruin them. Destroy them. They deserve it. We need to tarnish their reputations, cut them up into little pieces. And if you're not going to help me, fine, but I won't let you stop me!"

The vein in her forehead was throbbing, and I could see she wasn't going to listen to reason. As she was talking, I surreptitiously slid my hand over the keyboard and hit the Delete button.

"What did you do?" she screamed.

"I can't do this anymore," I pronounced, standing my ground. Enough was enough. Not matter how awful the Diamonds were.

"Move over!" she commanded, and pushed me off the chair. I fell to the floor as I watched her furiously type away on her computer, trying to retrieve the file.

She calmly turned and gave me the most horrible, evil smirk. In that exact moment she morphed from quasi-friend to demonic, fire-breathing emissary of Hades.

"Do you really think it's that easy to erase the file? You, on the other hand, are easy enough to erase now that I know what a loser backstabber you are. Get out!" she yelled in a virtually *Exorcist*-ian grunt.

"Sofia!"

"Get out!" she said, rising, grabbing me by the hair and opening the door. She literally threw me out of her room and slammed the door after me.

I was in shock. What now?

Chapter Twenty-Four

I was reeling, chest throbbing, head aching, and brow perspiring. I walked as fast as I could to the only ally I knew I had: Antony. I rang his room, but he wasn't there. I even meandered to the guy domain of soccer ("football") in the Entertainment Center in the common room, which was complete with upholstered couches, a snack bar, and a pool table. No Antony.

Some cricketeers walked in, and though I barely knew Moabi LeTroux, I decided to ask him if he by chance knew where Antony was.

"Antony? Oh, I think I saw Antony at the Cove."

"Where's that?" I asked.

Moabi and his friends laughed. "Love, I'll have to take you there sometime." He winked. What did that mean? *Ugh!* I exited the dorm in frustration and looked for him on the rugby field. No Antony. I ran up by the school store and main campus hall. The science lab center. The library. No Antony. I felt adrift. Alone. And exhausted. I didn't know where to go so I just wandered where my weary feet took me.

I found a small path that led to Lamoneaux, the tiny town adjacent to the campus; it was covered with winding stone streets, high on charm but low on "action," so not many of my school-mates seemed to venture there. Sofia had once dubbed it full of "townies," remarking that nary a Van Peltian hangs there since it is full of "bitter, jealous locals" who resented the exorbitant wealth of the students, adding to "town versus gown" tensions.

But in the wind-whipping cold of late October, I felt comfort in the tiny, homey alleyways. I looked up at the picturesque brick houses and felt a bit homesick, thinking of the families in the district as they started to prepare the evening's dinner. As I wandered down a stone-covered slope that led to the lake, I heard some music coming from a tiny tavern with a wrought-iron sign that looked like it had been there for centuries. It was called Le Ciel, which meant "the sky," and I immediately knew why the propri-etors had chosen this moniker: past the cozy main room with its wood-beamed ceiling and rustic lumber tables and floor, there was an outdoor porch overlooking the glistening water, and tons and tons of sky. It was breathtaking.

The quaint, rustic vibe soothed my tired bones and heart, and I was elated to see a table calling my name right in the center of the perfectly perched balcony. As I sat down and exhaled, I was stunned to see none other than Oliver at the corner table, alone with a textbook.

"Oliver!" I exclaimed, *so* happy to see a friendly face after an hour of solitary wandering.

"Hi there!" He smiled, making room for me as I impulsively headed over. "Lucy, what a surprise! I am so happy to see you."

"Me too."

"Listen, I feel . . . awful about intruding in your life earlier regarding Antony. It's truly none of my business, and—"

"Oliver, do not worry. You were concerned. That's what friends are for." I put my hand on his arm reassuringly.

He smiled and put his hand over mine. "Great, then."

"So, Oliver, I don't mean this in a cheesy-pickup-line way, but . . . come here often?"

He laughed. "Sometimes, Lucy, I feel like this is one of the few places around here that has a real soul to it."

"Well, I just got here, but that's my feeling exactly. I didn't even know it was here! It is so adorable, and charm is bursting from every little cobblestone and lantern!" I said, studying the half-crowded room of smiling, merry people.

"Well, some of our schoolmates don't exactly like to venture off their golden grids," he remarked with a half eye roll. "It's not exactly a velvet booth at Club Platinum with bottle service. If it's not somewhere on the jet-set circuit, they won't have it."

"I've noticed."

I was trying to reconcile his down-to-earth comment with Antony's version of Oliver. The two seemed like jigsaw puzzle pieces that didn't fit.

"Yeah, everyone is always concerned with the new hot place or club, or this 'in' spot. But this is old and weathered and real to me. And I've been coming here for two years, and literally not one other Van Peltian has darkened the doorway!"

"Well, it's their loss, then. I feel like this is the first mellow, laid-back air I've breathed since school started for me," I confessed.

"So how *do* you like school so far? I know it's kind of a unique place."

"*Unique*, yeah . . . that's one way to put it," I said, smiling.

"Do you not like it, then?"

"No, no, I do, it's just that . . . you know, the whole 'scene' isn't my whole thing."

"I have a secret for you," he said, leaning in conspiratorially. I was intrigued. "Mine neither."

I smiled, not really surprised. He seemed so laid-back, but then again he was royalty. I mean, he *was* the scene! Or at least the one everyone wanted to cavort with. "Really?" I asked. "'Cause it seems like the whole social world revolves around, you know, you and your gang."

"Do I have a gang?" he asked, amused. "Should I be wary of a drive-by shooting?"

"No." I laughed, realizing how silly I sounded. "I just mean your whole family and friends; you're wired. There's a network here. And I'm one of the small satellites not plugged in."

"I don't see that. You're just new, that's all. And if the catty social butterflies make you feel that way, well, then you make your own 'gang.'"

"I don't know, it's not as easy as it sounds. . . ."

"Lucy, now it's my turn to be 'cheesy': don't think these people are so great just because they have so-called glamorous lives. A lot of them are spoiled and boring. You, at least, have character."

I was just about to get a buzz from the flattery of his sincere and touching compliment when an acidic pit crept into my stomach. Was it good "character" to be the coconspirator in Sofia's crimes? A scholarship outsider who tried to spy into the lives of the rich and fabulous? What would Oliver think of me if he knew I was a semi-liaison to the coarse magazine that tracked his every move? I prayed he would never ever find out.

"I have an idea," Oliver offered, snapping me out of my reverie. "How about we share some fondue? Dominique, the owner, makes a killer pot. It might be a bullet to the heart, but it's almost worth it."

"I'm in," I said happily.

Chapter Twenty-Five

After our third shared bottle of Coca-Cola to wash down the indeed incredible fondue and toasted baguette, Oliver and I wandered back up the hill, out of Lamoneaux toward the campus. As we saw the imposing Gothic skyline of the school, a gust of icy wind enveloped us.

"I think that was the first kiss of winter," I said, shivering. "All the warmth of that delicious fondue just froze in my veins."

"Take this," said Oliver, whipping off his brown corduroy jacket and putting it over my shoulders before I could protest.

Could this guy really be a snob? He didn't know I was an army brat on a full ride to VP, but something about him made me think he truly wouldn't care.

As we walked in silence toward the dorms, the knot in my tummy grew with every pace.

"So, I quite enjoyed our little mini-marathon the other day. If you ever want to hit that track, I'm in. And you are one speed demon! I have to work my arse off to keep up with you!" he said.

"Yeah, right. I was keeping up with *you*," I corrected teasingly. "But yes, I'd love to be running buddies."

He stopped and smiled.

"Running buddies it is, then. Tomorrow morning at seven?"

"Done."

I nervously entered the dorm and ran straight to my room, luckily avoiding all contact with Sofia or anyone else, for that matter. It was dusk and I checked my email to see if Antony had written me; after my time with Oliver I realized I hadn't thought about him in a while and was feeling a bit guilty. Nada in my email box. I called his room.

"Hey there, lovely lady, I'm so sorry I missed you earlier. I was in the library," he said.

"Oh, that's weird. I went there looking for you. I must not have seen you."

"We're ships in the night. That's okay, I know you like to play hard to get. That's why I'm lucky to just hear your voice!"

"Oh, please," I said. "What are you doing?"

"I'm so knackered I was going to have dinner here with room service. But maybe we could meet later? I miss you, you know."

I miss you? Wow. No one had ever said that to me. I didn't even know if my mom said that to me when we talked. I was flattered, but also worried about all the homework that I had been ignoring in favor of tennis.

"I really, really want to see you but have to study. I haven't cracked a book all day."

"All right, then. I'll see you tomorrow. Sweet reading. And sweet dreams."

Ahhh, Antony!

I was happy to have touched base with him—just his confident tone set my mind at ease in that moment.

But still, in my princess bed with a majestic view of the burning pink setting sun, I was worried about what revenge Sofia had in store for me. That I had tried to delete the file clearly enraged her, but maybe she would come to her senses and get past it. I just had to keep my distance until it all blew over.

The next morning, when I reached the track, Oliver was stretching, waiting for me.

"I think you called it last evening, Lucy. It's definitely getting colder."

"Well, let's warm up and work off that cheese festival I taped to my ass," I lamented.

"Please do not tell me you're one of those girls fretting about their weight all the time."

"No!" *Yes.* Who didn't?

"Good. 'Cause that is so ridiculous to me! Especially when a girl looks great." Hmm, did that mean he thought I looked great? Interesting.

He bolted off before me and I sprinted to catch up. We had a lovely, though chilly, hour of sunrise running. Our matching pace let me know our minds were also in sync and that I had a friend.

The serene comfort I got from running with Oliver flew out the window when I entered my dorm and found Sofia standing at my door. She followed me into my room.

"So, how's your running pal, you little tramp? What happened to Antony?"

Her words were like daggers made of ice. Dipped in acid.

"Sofia, listen, Oliver and I are just friends—"

"Of course you are—it's not like he'd *ever* be into you! I know it's a tennis thing, but just seeing you try is so pathetic!"

"Sofia, why are you so mad? Does this have to do with the video?"

"Do you really think he'd ever go for you? You're a nobody. A scholarship army brat, *nobody.*"

Ouch.

"Sofia, what happened to 'My lips are sealed'?"

"Promises, shmomises! First you try to sabotage my files and now you're trying to social-climb the very people we had been try-ing to bust? Out for yourself now, aren't you? After all the time I put in showing you around, this is what I get in return? You mess with me and go off with the royals now."

"I'm not—I just—" My face reddened.

"You're a little bitch, Lucy, and I've got a CNN World News flash for you: you screwed with the wroooong girl when you tried to screw with my computer files. That was cold hard cash you almost deleted."

"Sofia, I—"

"There's nothing you can say to get out of this one. No tennis ball you can lob away your problems with. You're *over*, Wimbledon. You messed with me, and now you're toast."

Before slamming my door, she turned back to utter three short but deadly words. "This. Is. War."

Chapter Twenty-Six

The next few days were the worst in my life. I think I lost five pounds. Normally I would have been thrilled that now I had five pounds' worth of food I could eat (sweets preferably) in order to gain it back, but I had no appetite at all. I had never felt this level of acute, gut-churning stress. Initially I was anxious that Sofia would tell everyone about our prank. And then I was stressed about what tricks she would pull on me. And then I just became paranoid about everything. It was "Does that girl know?" or "Did that guy just look at me funny?" every time I walked down the hall.

The most horrible part was that I couldn't confess. I didn't want to tell anyone about the stuff we had done to the Diamonds because I was embarrassed, as well as worried that they would throw me out of school. I was also incredibly angry at myself for being so stupid! How could I have been involved in wiring another student's room so that a gossip magazine could get dirt on them? No matter how I played it, it was wrong. I was miserable. I knew if I called my sister, she would read me the riot act and tell my parents, who would have coronaries that their little angelic scholar-athlete had turned demonic. If I told Antony, I was sure he would think I was an evil brat who would go all *Fatal Attraction* on him if he crossed me. He wouldn't be able to get away fast enough. I was too ashamed to tell Oliver, though he seemed like he would offer good advice. And when I realized I had no one else to tell, I was depressed on top of scared. It was hopeless.

I had taken to darting around school. Rushing to class, rushing to practice, taking my meals in my room, and doing everything to minimize contact with anyone. I hadn't seen Sofia, and I felt both relief and fear. Was she locked up in her room plotting something? I was going insane! And to make things even worse, I could tell that Antony knew I was behaving oddly, but what could I do? After one really bad phone call, where he spent ten minutes trying to convince me to go to the pub with him and I spent that time pretending that I reeeeeally had to study for a test that I had *in two weeks*, I hung up the phone feeling defeated. How could I get out of this?

I was sitting in my room one day lamenting the situation, when suddenly there was a *ping* on my computer. I had an email. Phew. It was a message from Friend.

Looking pretty stressed out there. What's going on?

She noticed! It must be Rioko: I had just seen her in the hall that morning and she had given me a sympathetic nod. I felt like she was on my side. But could I trust her?

What do you do when you did something you really, really regret and it was so stupid and you wish you could take it back? Does that make sense? It's hard to explain. . . .

I pressed Send and waited. I sort of hoped that there would be an immediate knock at my door and Rioko would give me a hug and ask me what's up. Then I would download it all to her and she would come up with a great solution, and it would all be over and I could eat and sleep again.

Could you apologize to the person who did it? Surely they would be rational enough to accept your apology and move on. If not, they're not really worth having as a friend.

I quickly responded, with elevating desperation.

The thing is, they're not my friends. And they don't know that I did what I did. Sorry I'm being so cryptic, but it's complicated. I was stupid. I was angry at what someone said and then I exacted revenge upon them, when I should have just been a grown-up and moved on.

I pressed Send and waited. Out the window, I could see Victoria and Antigone clutching mugs of latte on the patio and laughing over something. If only I could be that carefree.

Okay, it's hard for me to give true advice because I don't know what you are talking about. But I would suggest the following: do everything you can to undo what you did first. Is there a way that they will never find out what you did if you can take it away beforehand? Second, straightforward honesty is usually the best way to go. It will be brutal at first, but after you suffer a bit (which I am sure will be better than the purgatory you appear to be in now), it will all blow over and you can move on. That's all I can think of without knowing more.

I thought about what Friend had written. It would be horrible to confess. I was sure the Diamonds would go to the head of the school. And what would I say? Yes, I was the lookout when Sofia wired their rooms. They would expel me for sure. But what if I took down the wires? That would be the first move to make it better. I could at least undo some of the damage. I'd have to think about a good reason for confession. At present, I saw no reason for them to forgive me. If only I had something that they wanted. Or could help them in some way. Tennis lessons anyone?

No, it still seemed hopeless.

I can undo part of it, but as for fessing up, not sure that's the right move. Future is at stake.

I quickly sent my response.

You know what you have to do. Good luck.

Ah, yes, Friend. I knew what I had to do. But was I brave enough?

Chapter Twenty-Seven

I waited until I heard the last door close. I had done something this morning that I never did (which was beginning to be a trend) and called in sick to tennis practice. Coach Sachs had uttered what I assumed were expletives in German and then promised that the makeup drills that I would be forced to do upon my return would be dire, but his words didn't even faze me. I had no choice. I had to have the dorm to myself so that I could remove the wires from the Diamonds' rooms and erase everything from Sofia's computer—for good, this time. It would be beyond risky, but I felt like I had no choice. Luckily there was a *crêpe fête* in the boys' dorm this morning, an annual tradition where the boys served the girls breakfast. Everyone would be there. And everyone who wasn't would be either at team practice or music rehearsals. That's just the way it was. So at 10:15, I walked out of my room to make my move.

I gently knocked at Victoria's door, knowing there would be no answer. My heart was beating so furiously I thought it would pop out. I slowly opened the door, looked around stealthily, and then ran over to the bed and extracted the little almost invisible wire that Sofia had placed above it. Quick as a mouse, I was in and out. I closed the door, glanced furtively around, then breathed a sigh of relief. Done. That was easy. God must have been on my side, because Iman's room was just as fast, and after a brief moment in Antigone's where I almost couldn't yank the wire out and thought I was doomed, I was able to extract it and get out of there before I heard a maid strolling down the hall.

Phew. Already I felt better. But now was the hard part. I had to go on Sofia's computer and erase the files. That would not be easy.

I knocked on her door. Silence. I knew she'd be at the *crêpe fête* mining scoops for her magazine. She wouldn't miss a chance to take note of some Irish heiress spilling maple syrup all over herself if she could get paid for reporting it. It was seeping in how dirty and rotten she was.

I hastily made my way over to the computer and turned it on.

It seemed to take eons for it to boot up, but it was probably only seconds. As soon as all the icons came on the screen I leaned in, desperate to find which one held the key to the files of all of the Diamonds prancing around their rooms. I saw a folder titled "Term Paper" and one called "Correspondence" and another "Maths." Hmm. Suddenly I heard footsteps out in the hall.

I didn't know what the hell to do. I panicked. I hastily jumped into Sofia's closet and waited. God, this was torture! I was so angry at myself. But the footsteps continued on down the hall, so I furtively opened the closet door and glanced out. The coast was clear. I ran over to the computer and started looking at file names. "Dissected Fairy Tales," "Earth Science I," "Islands of the World," "Ethics." Everything just looked like homework. Where could it be? I kept flipping through until it suddenly dawned on me. Ethics? Sofia would never take an ethics class. She had no ethics! I opened the folder and quickly enough video of Iman's room appeared, followed by those of the other Diamonds. Bingo! I immediately dragged the folder to the Trash and then emptied it, and also searched for any backup files. I hoped that would do the trick.

I turned off the computer, making sure I erased everything that would let her know I had been on it, and was about to leave her room when something on her desk caught my eye. I was stunned; under her copy of *Crime and Punishment* was a folder with my name, Lucy A. Peterson, typed on the side. Inside were all of my records, including my parents' financial statement, my essay to get into the school, my entire application, even recommendations from former teachers. With her Golden Key membership she'd somehow gotten access to the Records Office and had stolen my file.

Now I was in a quandary. I couldn't leave it. God knows what she would do with it. I was both scared and furious that she was able to get her hands on this. What else did she have in her possession?

My mind was racing, but it suddenly stopped and everything became clear. I knew what I had to do. I had to face her.

Forty-five minutes later, Sofia opened the door. I could see that she was surprised at first, but her astonishment was quickly replaced with anger. She furrowed her brow and practically spat out her words: "What the hell are you doing in my room?"

Chapter Twenty-Eight

"I know you're mad, but we have to work through this," I said, trying to stay calm and unemotional. That was key in tennis—never let them see you sweat. I was, in fact, soaked, but remained visibly cool.

"You don't know anything! Get out," she said icily. I remained standing in my spot as if iron bolts held my feet to the carpet. *"Get the hell out!"*

"I'm not leaving until we talk this through. I took down the wires I was complicit in installing. If you want to sabotage these people, that is your problem. But regardless of what they did to me, I don't care anymore. If they're rude and evil, then they'll dig their own graves, but I can't have a hand in taking them down."

I braced myself, but Sofia one-upped me in coolness. A cold laugh emanated from her red lips. It grew louder and louder, totally rattling me.

"Oh, you kill me! You Americans are so damn righteous! How sad. You really think you have to always take the high road in life, such stars in your eyes. Justice! Righteousness! You're pathetic. Get out of my room this instant."

"Why do you have my file? That is my property. Or the school's, but certainly not yours."

"Ooooh, what are you going to do, tattle?"

"Maybe."

"Go ahead! I'll deny everything and say you did it. My tuition is paid in full. In cash. I think this file reveals yours is not. Hence, you would gain the most from these capers and working for *Gab!* magazine. My dad will personally get on the phone and say you were the contact."

"You wouldn't dare!" I cried. Obviously her father had taught her well; she was a second-generation scumbag.

"Oh yes I would. Just try to mess with me again and you'll regret it."

She opened the door and gestured for me to exit, which I did, in silence, holding my file, which I planned to put back in the main office. Not that she hadn't xeroxed everything already, I was sure. Back in my room I found an email from Friend.

How's it going? Thinking of you & hope everything's OK. . . .

I wrote back:

Losing energy. I think new strategy is to hide the rest of the term.

Seconds later:

These things always work themselves out. When people are hurtful, they get their just deserts.

Hmm . . . a kernel of wisdom. I hoped she was right. I hoped it would all go away. I prayed.

Chapter Twenty-Nine

*A*ntony valiantly fought to retrieve me from my wallowing state.

"I've never heard of anyone studying so much here! Time to live a bit! We also must go shopping for your gown tomorrow." We were strolling through the campus's rolling country hills, and he took my hand and kissed it.

Gown? "What are you talking about?"

"For the Winter Ball!"

Of course. The Winter Ball. Even as I roamed zombielike in

my daze I had gleaned a few things about this famous event. The Winter Ball was like a prom, times ten. Supposedly there were even horse-drawn carriages. It was a white-tie extravaganza with an all-night feast.

"It's the last event before we all leave for Christmas and then go to the Gstaad campus," Antony explained. "It's like a farewell of sorts to this place."

"Gosh, I feel like we just got here!" I exclaimed.

"Gstaad is lovely. Quite romantic."

He pulled me in and kissed me. It felt warm and nice, but I was still so closed off.

"Also, I never officially asked you, but . . . " Antony took my hands in his. "Will you be my date for the Winter Ball?"

"Of course. . . . " I blushed a bit but still had the lump in my throat from my face-off with Sofia. It's hard to relax when you know someone has made a declaration of war against you.

"So shall we go to Geneva tomorrow for the day so you can buy your dress?" he asked.

Was he kidding?

"Yeah, right," I said sarcastically. As if I could walk into Chanel and walk out with a five-thousand-dollar gown!

"Oh, why yes, naturally," said Antony. "You probably wear couture and had it made for you already in Paris."

"Exactly," I said, rolling my eyes.

Across the field, I saw Oliver and Maxwell walking back from the tennis courts. They were engaged in conversation, with Oliver gesticulating with great animation. Suddenly I felt a weird ache and wished it were *me* and not Maxwell talking to him.

With the Winter Ball, the escort was the all-important key. Everyone had to have a date—no one went stag. While it was nice to have Antony ask me, I couldn't help but wonder who Oliver would be taking—not that he would have asked me.

Chapter Thirty

The next afternoon at tennis, Coach Sachs ran through the seed list in preparation for the upcoming game. I was still seeded number one and I was thrilled, but I could feel Victoria's hostile eyes burrowing into my back. It didn't help when Maxwell made a big deal of calling me "Number One" in practice instead of his usual "Venus." The coach further explained that in the spring, when we started the season in earnest, we would have matches every weekend. I'd heard we didn't stay at the schools we played against but in lavish hotels, and we'd be flown on one of the school's private planes! I'd be away all the time, and I couldn't wait. The thought was getting me through the creepy, nervous time tiptoeing around school.

It was no surprise I liked to wander off campus. Antony had suggested I meet him in the library when I finished tennis practice, but as I walked toward the looming Gothic building, my legs suddenly started moving in a different direction, farther and farther down the stone path to the front gates of Van Pelt, down the windy cobblestone street into Lamoneaux. As I rounded the corner that led to Le Ciel, I could hear the din of happy-hour carousers and could see smoke from the chimney as the November fires warmed the tavern guests.

Inside, my heart began to race as I made my way through the main room while music played and revelers toasted the end of the workday. Finally my eyes found what they were looking for, what my legs had walked themselves here for: Oliver.

"Hey, Lucy," said Oliver.

He wasn't his usual cheerful self, and for a moment I thought he was less than thrilled to see me.

"Sit down," he said.

His scruffy hair, crystal blue eyes, and perfect face had a weathered, almost melancholy aura.

"I never thought I'd say this to you, especially since I'm the social train wreck here, but are you okay?" I ventured.

"Yeah, sure, I suppose," he said, but then he continued. "Life is just sometimes bollocks, you know?"

"True," I said. "What sort of bollocks are we talking about today?"

"Oh, just my father. He . . . " Oliver paused. "He's angry that I'm seeded third in tennis."

"Well, it's all subject to change," I said reassuringly. "And it's not like you need to be the best tennis player to pay for college."

Oliver gave me a curious look.

"You know, my dad rides me about ranking in tennis, but it's because it's my golden ticket. I need to get a scholarship to get into college," I said, not really believing I was revealing all this to Oliver.

"Yeah, I guess I am very lucky that way."

"I didn't mean to undermine your feelings. But you should just do your best out there—which you do—and then try not to worry as much about your father."

"It's all I can do, right?" He shrugged and took a swig of his cider.

It seemed a crime that Oliver could be so upset! No one was nicer, sweeter, or more . . . handsome. "Oliver, this is so not major. Does your father know the more important things, like that everyone wants to be friends with you, to *be* you? And that you're so nice to everyone even though you more than anyone would have the right to be snobby?"

Oliver raised his eyes in amusement. "Tell me how you really feel, Lucy," he said, and finally smiled.

"It's true, though. Sometimes people have to be told the

obvious. You're a great guy. Don't let your father's disappointment about something so petty freak you out."

"You're right," he said, staring at me intently.

Suddenly I felt as if I had said too much. But I was glad that I had.

"I know one thing that might make you feel better, though it's just a Band-Aid. A Band-Aid with lots of calories?"

He smiled. "I like how you think, Lucy." He flagged down the proprietress. "Dominique, how about some of your incredible fondue, *s'il vous plaît?*"

"*Absolument*, Oliver!" she said, batting her eyelashes.

Now that Oliver seemed to be in a better mood, and since I was feeling more comfortable, I decided to bring up something that had been bothering me.

"Now that you know I think you're a fine fellow, I do want to ask you something, but please tell me if I'm being too nosy or offensive," I began.

"Uh-oh," he said.

"No, don't worry. It's . . . The only reason I ask is because it just doesn't seem *you*. You're not the type. . . . " I said, stalling and stumbling for words.

"What is it, already?" he asked with a smile.

"I, um, saw a picture of you in a magazine at a soccer—er, I mean football—game, and it said you had caused a riot or something. I know it's not my place. I just thought it totally didn't sound like you and I wondered what happened."

Oliver grimaced and I instantly wished I hadn't brought it up.

"Sorry, none of my beeswax," I said hastily, taking a sip of my drink.

"No, it's . . . it's okay," he said haltingly. "That was just a very embarrassing moment. I really hate when I lose my temper. And I never want to do anything to humiliate my family," he said, brow furrowed.

"Okay . . . ," I said meekly, trying to think of a way to change the topic.

"No, I'm glad you asked, because it really made me seem like a spoiled little wanker, and I'm not like that at all," he said, finally smiling.

"Yeah, I know! That's why I brought it up."

"There were two blokes and they just kept egging us on, saying crude things, taunting us. I lost my cool when they threw a cup of soda at my younger sister. I know I shouldn't have, but animal instincts, I suppose. . . . "

How heroic! It was the answer I wanted, the answer I secretly knew I would get. Oliver had been chivalrous, a knight in shining armor protecting his little sis. It was so romantic.

"Gosh, that's horrible. People can be so evil."

"I know," he said, putting his hands on the table. "But, anyway, I overreacted. I should have just walked away. But I duly paid the piper and I'm glad it's behind me."

"Don't you wish you could tell your side of the story?" I asked.

"Sometimes you just need to put things behind you."

There was a pause while Oliver looked off into the distance. I watched him, embarrassed that I had said anything.

"Sorry I brought it up."

"No, Lucy, I'm glad you did. It's important to me that you know that I'm not that type of bloke. I try to be a good guy."

He smiled and all I can say is what they say in romance novels: we shared a moment. Moments later the waitress brought over our fondue and we focused on dipping baguettes and crisp vegetables into Dominique's iron cauldron of bubbling cheese. It was, in a word, heaven. Oliver looked up from his cheese explosion and smiled at me, and I felt like everything was okay. This place truly was magical.

Chapter Thirty-One

Oliver walked me all the way back to my dorm, and I floated up the stairs with a giant grin on my face. Suddenly a thought seized me: maybe Oliver liked me. It sounded crazy in theory, but the fact was we always had amazing conversations and it seemed like we both, not just me, sought out each other's company. I mean, I know I had Antony and Oliver had Angelina, but maybe we were meant for each other?

The thought got me through dinner (which I still ate despite the pig-out with Oliver) and homework that night. It was the first time in days that I didn't stress about Sofia. I had some weird optimism seizing my body. In my fuzzy daydreams, Oliver and I were laughing and giggling, arm in arm, on the streets of London and having "family dinners" with the queen. It could be possible—why not? The question was, what to do about Antony? I'd been spending less and less time with him lately since I'd been holing myself up in my room, avoiding Sofia, and to be honest, I hadn't missed him that much. Hmm.

The next morning started off sensationally. I was thrilled to have aced a pop quiz in my terrorism class, and was even more excited that Angelina Jolie was the guest speaker in our human rights class. She spoke so eloquently of the crimes against humanity in third-world countries that even the boys were in tears. Though maybe they were crying because she was taken by Brad Pitt. Everything was going my way until I got to tennis practice and found Victoria standing in front of my locker. One look at her and it was clear she was irate.

"Did you spread bad rumors about me being anorexic and passing out after parties?" she demanded, steam practically blowing out her ears.

"No," I answered, shaking my head, though I was sure Sofia was behind this.

"Because I heard from a very reliable source that it was *you*."

"Victoria, I swear, I didn't. I have a feeling I know who said it, but I don't think it's right to say anything and get into a huge he-said-she-said."

Suddenly, out of nowhere, Victoria slapped me across the face. *Hard.* And just as she did, the school physical therapist, Mademoiselle Behar, rounded the corner and saw her do it.

"Victoria!" screamed Mademoiselle Behar.

Victoria seemed surprised to see Mademoiselle Behar, but even more surprised by what she had done. Tears shot to my eyes and I could feel my face stinging. Victoria took a step back.

"How could you do that?" asked Mademoiselle Behar, still aghast.

"I, um . . . "

For once, Victoria looked scared. It was outlined clearly in every single Van Pelt rule book that violence would not be tolerated and would result in immediate dismissal. It supposedly went back to the day when Idi Amin's son and one of the Fiat heirs got into a giant fistfight that resulted in major lawsuits. Drinking, smoking, and all that other stuff would be judged case by case, but one fight and you were out the door. Zero tolerance.

"It's okay, Mademoiselle Behar, we were just practicing a skit for our terrorism class. Victoria really got into character, but we're all good," I said, touching my cheek. I tried to smile, but my face was still stinging.

Mademoiselle Behar's eyes narrowed in disbelief. Victoria, still stunned, just stood there, speechless.

"Okay," said Mademoiselle Behar finally. "But I don't think it's a good idea to be so rough."

"We won't be next time!" I said fake cheerily.

I waited while Mademoiselle Behar walked away, and I heard the door to the locker room close. Victoria turned and looked at me.

"I don't know why I did that. . . . " she said. "I guess . . . I don't know. Why did you defend me? You could have had me out on my rump."

"Look," I said, "it's insane that you think you can treat me the same way Naomi Campbell treats her maids, but I don't see any reason to get the teachers or administration involved in this." I didn't want to say "Because I wired your room and I helped get your bracelet into a gossip magazine." Better not to open up that can of worms. "I think that we should stop being enemies. We're teammates. We don't have to be friends, but we should at least be cordial. No slapping." I said the last part as an attempt to lighten the mood.

Then we both got quiet for a minute and I could tell she was debating how to move on.

"Wow, you have a giant handprint on your face. I'm terribly sorry," she finally said.

"It's okay."

Suddenly Victoria smiled. "You know, you're kind of all right."

"Thanks," I said before I walked out to the courts.

Chapter Thirty-Two

*P*ractice went well. It was weird, a whole different vibe, and I could tell everyone picked up on it. Victoria didn't make any of her usual bitchy remarks, and it was like a domino effect because Maxwell didn't make any of his usual rude and inappropriate comments. Angelina and Oliver seemed surprised that the frost was melting, and I could tell that everyone was genuinely relieved. We were all in much better moods. And afterward, Victoria and I walked down the hill, and we even started *bonding*. We made fun of the coach—and since she had a German accent she could do a dead-on impersonation. It was kind of fun.

But the next day, when I was getting ready for afternoon practice (since there was a game coming up, Coach had upped the practices to two a day,) there was a knock on my door and Victoria, Antigone, and Iman were on the threshold.

"What's up, guys?" I asked nervously. I could tell they were not happy.

"Can we have a word with you, please?" asked Iman, barging in.

"Sure."

I stared at each girl. Only Victoria looked a little ill at ease.

"What's up?" I asked again, putting my hand on my desk chair as if to brace myself.

"Sofia told us that the reason you guys are not bosom buddies anymore is because you were stealing from her and everyone," said Antigone, her slight Greek accent drawing out the word *bosom* to be like *booooosom*.

"That's a lie," I said, my face getting red.

"Is it?" asked Iman, folding her arms.

"I have never stolen. Ever. Feel free to search my room," I said, waving my arm around.

"We will," said Iman.

Suddenly I realized something and I felt like I would faint. I knew it. Of course they would find stuff, but it would be stuff that Sofia had *planted* there. In fact, now that I thought about it, I remembered that last night when I had gotten back I noticed my sweatshirt was on the chair, when I knew I had thrown it on the floor in my haste to get to the shower.

"Guys, I swear, anything you find in here Sofia put there herself. I would never steal," I said.

"We just have to make sure," said Victoria softly.

"Of course," I said gallantly. I was trying to put on my honest face. It sucks when you are telling the truth and you want everyone to know it, and then it looks like you are trying too hard and not telling the truth. Like when I go through U.S. Customs and they ask me if I have anything illegal or am bringing in any weapons and I am totally not, but I start thinking, Maybe I am. Maybe someone slipped drugs into my suitcase. Then I get all panicky and sweaty.

Iman immediately set about opening every single drawer in my desk and my bureau. Victoria stood behind her, and I could tell she was conflicted about whether or not she should partake. Antigone started to look under my bed.

"It's okay, guys, I have nothing to hide," I said, whipping open my closet doors so that they could see everything I owned.

"Where're the rest of your clothes?" Victoria asked, horrified.

"That's all I have."

"No way!" said Iman, putting her hand up to her mouth to suppress a laugh. "Pathetic!"

Iman got back to work, opening drawer after drawer.

"Come on, Iman, enough," said Victoria finally.

"Not so fast," said Iman. She turned around and held up a pair of ruby earrings. "You bloody thief! My father gave these to me!"

"Iman—," I began.

"I was looking for them everywhere! I couldn't find them yesterday!" said Iman, literally kissing her earrings.

"How could you?" asked Victoria, truly disappointed.

"Iman, I swear to you that before this minute I never laid eyes on them. It's clear that Sofia put them there."

"As if," said Antigone.

A calm suddenly seized me. "Iman, when did you last have those earrings? Can we go through the timeline?"

"I wore them yesterday morning, and then I took them off when I went to fencing practice. When I got back in the afternoon they were gone!" she said. "You are so busted."

"Wait a minute," I said, buying time. "Yesterday afternoon? Okay, I have an alibi! I was at the pub in Lamoneaux."

"Lamoneaux? Ew! It's all townies there," said Victoria in disgust.

"Do you really want us to believe you were there?" asked Iman.

"I was, I swear!"

"I don't know," said Antigone, staring at Iman doubtfully. But who in their world would admit they had been in Lamoneaux? I *had* to be telling the truth in their eyes.

"She'll probably pay off some drunk local to confirm her story," said Iman. "People, please! It's a lie! She's a liar!"

"Did anyone else see you there?" asked Victoria finally.

"Yes."

"Who?" said the Diamonds in unison.

I didn't want to tell them. If I did, everyone would know our special place, our special secret. I would ruin Lamoneaux for Oliver and myself. It might become *trendy* because he went there. Popular. Could I?

"I really don't want to say. . . . "

"You have to," said Antigone sternly.

I felt like I was selling my soul to the devil.

"Who was with you?" asked Victoria. I felt like her voice was echoing in my head.

"Yes, tell us," said Iman.

I had no choice. "Oliver," I said as softly as I could. As soon as I said it, I felt as if I had given up the biggest secret of my life. But I had no choice. *Forgive me, Oliver!*

Chapter Thirty-Three

The trio blew out of my room, on an Oliver manhunt for alibi verification, presumably. I knew he would be in his dorm, getting ready for tennis practice, where I was due shortly. Antigone and Iman seemed enraged, but I knew I'd connected with Victoria and established at least a modicum of trust.

A half hour later, when I arrived at tennis practice, Oliver strolled over with a huge grin on his face. "Didn't take you for the cat burglar type, Luce," he teased. "Don't worry, I told them you were too busy clogging your arteries to nab Iman's earrings."

I was relieved he clearly knew the whole escapade was a total fabrication. "Ugh, can you believe this? It's a long story, but—"

"It's not that long," he said. "It's one word actually: *Sofia*."

"How did you know?" I asked.

"I surmised. The first few weeks of school I noticed you with her a lot. There's something about her I can't quite put my finger on, but it's dishonest." He had her number, and he didn't even know about the magazine connection or my apprenticeship in tabloid trash. "You, on the other hand, just seem . . . good to me, Lucy. I don't know, I didn't see you two together."

He drifted off in thought. I was about to ask him what was going through his head when Coach Sachs interrupted.

"Hey! Oliver, court two, volleys. And you, Lucy, I need to see nonstop serves."

Just as I walked over to my side of the court, Victoria rushed in from the ladies' locker room.

"You're late. Get to work!" shouted Coach sternly.

"I was here. I just had to use the bathroom—," she began, but Coach stopped her and pointed to a spot across the net.

Victoria nodded and came up next to me where I was practicing. She gave me a sideways look, as if she were still assessing everything that went down.

"Oliver confirmed," she said finally, throwing her ball in the air before smashing it across the court.

"I know," I said.

"Quit your gabbing!" yelled Coach from across the net. "It's not teatime, it's practice."

We obeyed and hit our serves. I watched Angelina across the way and wondered if she had heard everything that was going on and if so, what she thought. She seemed like the type who wouldn't really care. Although maybe she did; I didn't know. She was definitely a tough nut to crack.

After Coach called an end to practice, Victoria and Angelina wandered down to the dorms, and I decided to stay and hit, out-lasting the boys and even the daylight. As the sun's rays turned to pink and orange, goose bumps rose on my skin and I knew it was time to head back.

When I walked off the court, Antony was there waiting for me. Seeing his big blue eyes made me feel very guilty about my feelings for Oliver.

"Are you avoiding me?" he asked, wounded.

"No, not at all," I said, trying to seem casual. "I just have been so crazed with stuff—"

"Well, we're still going to Winter Ball together, right?"

"Yes, of course. . . . " I felt awful. I repeated in my head the mantra: *Go for the guy who likes you, go for the guy who likes you. . . .*

"I just feel like you've been MIA lately," Antony said.

"No no no no," I protested. "I just have been, you know, stressed."

"Okay, then. Well, I have to go work, but why don't we have dinner tomorrow?"

"Sure, sounds great."

"You know, Lucy," he said, taking my hands, "I can't stop thinking about you." Sigh. He was so romantic I couldn't help getting caught up.

"Me too," I said. "I've missed you."

As he walked away, my cheese-dunking with Oliver seemed like a faraway daydream—Oliver was a friend, yes, but I knew he could never be mine, so I had to stop fantasizing and live in reality. And Antony was it.

Chapter Thirty-Four

"Okay, so we owe you an apology."

I heard Iman's voice at my door as I turned to find all three Diamonds—Antigone, Iman, and Victoria—standing in the frame of the paneled portal.

"Come on in," I said, getting up. "Don't worry about it."

Antigone spoke first. "Sofia is a snake! She must have taken our stuff. She's the thief."

"What else has she been up to?" said Iman, plopping down on my bed and flipping through a tennis magazine that I had been reading.

I gulped. Luckily it was a rhetorical question.

"She's going to get it," said Victoria. "I already told Maxwell that Sofia has some weird medical condition. He's such a gossip, everyone will know by the end of the day!"

"Perfect," said Antigone.

Wow, this was Sofia's worst nightmare. But she deserved it for what she did to them.

"Anyway, we know now you're truthful," said Iman, rising. "So, you're cool with us."

"Thanks," I said.

"And Oliver said you're funny and nice and a great pal," said Victoria.

Hmm . . . funny and nice? Pal? Definitely not lovey-dovey terms, more like asexual sisterly ones. But that was even better because it brought a dose of reality to my life and put an immediate end to my royal reveries.

"So, see you around," said Antigone.

Then all three of the Diamonds got up and left the room.

I was so relieved I had gotten the stamp of approval from the Diamonds that when I got to practice a little late the next morning (meaning not early as usual), I blithely skipped up to Oliver and tapped him with my racket. "Hey there!" I was now very Zen about his brother-type role. I'd always wanted a big brother, and I felt I could truly trust him and that we were on the same wavelength.

Except for some reason my friendly greeting garnered no response.

"Oliver?"

Oliver barely met my eye. "Oh, hey, Luce. How's it going?"

It was the first time he seemed like he didn't actually care what my response was.

"It's been *crazy*."

But before I could continue Oliver interrupted me. "Cool, okay, gotta do my laps," he said, before dashing off around the court, leaving me standing alone and speechless. I watched him rush over to Angelina and say something to her before they both started laughing.

I couldn't help but feel paranoid. Were they laughing at me? What had happened? Had I done something wrong?

Chapter Thirty-Five

I was stressed about Oliver. Why was he being weird? I wished I had someone to confide in. Sofia was now in the enemy category. The Diamonds and I were just starting to be civil, so it would be weird to bring this up. I suppose I could tell Antony, but it would be a little odd to talk to him about another guy. I think he would wonder why I cared so much. I guess I should wonder also. I was hoping to get a little advice from Friend, but she had remained silent for the past few days, so I was left to my own devices. I felt very friend*less*. Finally I decided that

I should just bite the bullet and go down the hall and seek out Rioko's friendship. She was clearly Friend, so why have this facade? Maybe we could actually interface beyond the cyber world.

The violin stopped after I knocked on the door, and seconds later Rioko was standing on the threshold.

"Hi, Lucy."

"Hi, Rioko, can I come in for a sec?"

"Sure," she said.

Her room was immaculate, which I guess wasn't hard because we had twenty-four-hour maid service, but still. On her wall she had posters of famous musicians and composers, and her entire double-wide armoire was bursting with her practice materials, including music stands, sheets of music, and all sorts of violin paraphernalia. Who knew that violinists needed so much stuff?

Rioko motioned for me to sit down, a little awkwardly, and I did. It was funny, because she was not someone you would notice in general, in class or walking down the hall. She sort of made a point of disappearing into the walls. But when you actually looked closely at Rioko, you could see that behind her glasses she had sparkling eyes, beautiful dimpled cheeks, and the most perfect creamy skin. She was actually a knockout.

"So, how's your history paper coming along?" I asked, making conversation.

"Oh, yes, good. I finished it this weekend," she said modestly.

"Already? Oh my gosh, that's amazing! You are way ahead of

the curve," I said, impressed.

She looked down at her toes. I'm sure she was wondering if I realized she was Friend and wanted to cut to the chase.

"Listen, Rioko, I am assuming it's you who has been sending me those emails. And I just want to say that I totally appreciate it. They have really made my day and gotten me through some tough times. But you haven't been online lately—most likely jamming on your paper—and I thought maybe we could talk in person. Because I really need your advice."

She suddenly appeared confused. "Emails? You mean when I asked you for the homework?"

"No, I mean . . . aren't you 'Friend'?"

She smiled. "I consider you a friend, Lucy. I don't have many. . . . "

"No, I mean, don't you send me those anonymous emails cheering me up and giving me advice? Don't you sign off as 'Friend'?" If it wasn't Rioko, who could it be?

But Rioko shook her head. "Sorry, Lucy. It's not me."

I was devastated. All along I had thought she was the one. Who would know that the Diamonds were doing something to my door? Who would offer nice advice? Not Sofia. It had to be someone in the dorm, right? But who?

"No, I'm sorry. I just assumed it was you. But no problem," I added quickly.

"Okay," she said. I could tell she was a little puzzled.

"Listen, I really do want to be your friend. I don't have many!"

Rioko's face brightened. "Me either! I feel like the biggest nerd in the school. I mean, I know that musicians are considered nerds, but everyone here seems so . . . cool."

I looked at her and suddenly we both started laughing. Hysterically. And for the next hour we chatted and gossiped and had the best time. Once she opened up, it was as if every thought and opinion and observation just came rushing out of her. And Rioko was *funny*. She had a very simple way of describing people that was brutally honest without being mean.

I told her as much as I could about the last couple of days—not the details about what Sofia and I had done, but that we'd had a falling-out. I even told her about the Diamonds searching my room and finally realizing that Sofia had planted Iman's earrings. It all came rushing out. And she was the right person to tell. The Diamonds had been mean to her also, and she could not stand Sofia, which I thought was funny. She saw through everything. When I got to Oliver, she oohed and aahed over him as I did. But her last comment cut me to the heart.

"I totally sympathize with you, Lucy, but you know that Oliver is taken."

I gulped. I knew it but didn't know it. "Angelina?"

"Yeah, I'm so sorry. I heard that he asked her to the Winter Ball ages ago."

Ages ago? That stung. So I never had a chance. Why did I care? I had Antony.

"I shouldn't care. I have Antony."

Rioko nodded sympathetically. "And he's a good guy to you?"

"I think so, why? Do you know something?"

I could tell Rioko was contemplating whether or not to tell me something. She looked off in the distance, then chose her words carefully. "I don't know, Lucy. I mean, you would know better, I don't know. But . . . "

"But what?"

"I don't know. I always see him hanging out with that girl who works in the store, you know, the one with the va-va-va-vooms."

Chérie. "I saw them also."

"But maybe they're just friends," she quickly added.

"Maybe. But maybe it's time he and I have another conversation about her."

"Sorry, Lucy."

"Don't worry. I like to get everything out in the open. I'll ask him tomorrow."

Chapter Thirty-Six

But I didn't get a chance to see Antony the next day. I had planned on going to the caffè after classes to find him, but as I was walking down the hall of the dorm Iman saw me pass and called me into her room. Victoria and Antigone were in there also, both casually sitting on the floor cross-legged, looking through old magazines.

"Hey there," they said casually.

I wondered if I had been called in for a reason.

"So what is the deal with Sofia? Did you hear anything?" asked Victoria.

"She's been quiet lately. She turns the other way if she sees me and glares at me across the lunchroom. I'm scared at what she may be planning," I confessed. It had been really worrying me lately. It was not like Sofia to make herself invisible.

"Don't worry, we'll take care of her," said Victoria with confidence.

"Anyway, Lucy, we were just talking about you," Antigone said, and the other girls glanced at her and nodded.

Okay . . . "What's up?"

"We decided that we think we should be friends," said Iman, as if she were granting me a Nobel Prize.

"Yeah, we think we could add another Diamond," said Antigone. "A junior one."

"An apprentice," said Iman quickly.

At first I was truly flattered, and very excited. *They want me to be their friend! YAY! The cool girls.* But then I had to take a deep breath and really think about this. I had done some bad stuff to them, but they had been really mean and nasty to me. And to Rioko, who was now my only friend.

"Guys," I began. "Until now you've not been very nice to me. You really hurt Rioko's feelings when you laughed through her violin recital in Assembly. And it's not cool doing petty things to people like not letting them sit with you at the lunch table. I was new and felt like a nerd when you did that. Not to mention making fun of my clothes, and who can forget the redecoration of my door?"

"But it didn't seem like you cared!" said Victoria, astonished.

"You come in here, take *my* place on the tennis team, become BFFs with Oliver, the most sought-after boy at the school, and act all casual like it's nothing!"

"First off, it's not my fault about tennis. I feel bad that I took your spot, but I'm just trying to play my best."

"I know, but I worked hard for number one!" said Victoria.

"Who knows, Victoria, it can all change! As far as I know you can take private lessons with Steffi Graf this summer and become number one next year."

"Boris Becker," she said quietly.

"See, I'm not taking lessons with a pro! You have the upper hand."

"True," said Antigone. "It's not her fault."

"And as far as sitting at the table, I mean, hello? I'm new here. I don't know the routine. And I only had Sofia to teach me the ropes, and we all know how that turned out."

We all laughed.

"And about Oliver . . . I think he's my friend, but he's a hard one to read. . . . "

"I know, isn't he?" asked Iman. "So friendly one second and reserved the next."

"I think his family puts a lot of pressure on him," explained Victoria. "I think it's hard for him to let himself be totally care-free."

"But, God, is he hot!" Antigone giggled.

"Gorgeous," said Victoria.

"Smokin'!" I chimed in.

Before we knew it, we had dissolved into fits of girlish laughter. Once they let their guard down, they actually weren't half bad. Most of their attitude seemed to be a pretense, and they'd been impressed with how I stood up to them. We talked things out, and the Diamonds agreed to apologize to Rioko and to try not to torture newbies. It was the beginning of a beautiful friendship. . . .

Chapter Thirty-Seven

There had been a lot of flux in the friendship department and I couldn't believe the current state of affairs. I was now enemies with Sofia and friends with the Diamonds. Oliver was keeping me at bay, but at the same time, Angelina was being really nice. She'd asked me to study with her one night in the dorm, and we even had pizza another night. It was all confusing.

Ultimately I decided to switch off all the personal stuff and keep my eyes on the prize: winning the upcoming match. I spent all my time on the courts, and Coach Sachs fired balls at me until

I thought I'd pass out. I had tunnel vision, smashing that yellow furry orb with everything I had. I was on fire! Nothing could stop me! Nothing . . . but Oliver. The only thing that broke my focus was looking around when he was in the vicinity. He was still acting weird. I didn't even care that he was going to the Winter Ball with Angelina—at that point I just missed him as an ally, a pal I could plop down with at Le Ciel and just be myself. Sometimes I thought he was the only person I'd truly connected with and who I felt at ease with in my own skin, without judgments.

After practice one day I said hi to him and got a tepid response. I was so fed up, wondering what I'd done to merit this, that I went back to my dorm and called my sister.

Amanda and I had not really talked all that much lately. We were superclose back home, but I felt like ever since I'd been accepted here, she'd kind of been snippy and judgmental. I knew it was partly jealousy, but also partly that she was worried I would become a spoiled brat. It was a bummer, because my life was so different and I really did need to share it with her. Yes, the guys she talked about were mostly soldiers from the base, and the guys I referred to were princes and counts, but it was still the same set of issues.

"Hey," I said when she answered the phone. "It's me."

"Hey, Luce, how's it going?"

"Things are fine, how are you?"

I wanted her to be the first to talk. Luckily she'd just been out with a guy the night before who had taken her to a fancy Italian restaurant and bought her red roses, so she was really psyched and in a good mood.

"So what's up with you?" she asked after giving me the full details about the new man.

"Nothing much. . . . " I said.

"Come on, how's that guy you like?"

"Antony?" I asked.

"No, I don't think that was his name . . . Oliver," she said.

"I didn't say I liked him," I protested.

"Ah, but a sister always knows. So what's the deal with him?"

I launched into the whole saga, how he was such a good friend and now he was acting weird. I even confided about the Diamonds and told her some of the stuff about Sofia, but not all (I didn't want to worry her—besides, it was hopefully all over). I mentioned Antony and Chérie, and everything else as well, and when I was done there was a pause.

"Sounds like you need to reach out to Oliver again," she advised.

"But what if he thinks I'm a dork?" I asked. "Besides, it's his turn to try to make an overture to me."

"Don't be like that. If he's a genuine friend—despite the fact that you are madly in love with him—you want to see what's going on. Write him a letter."

"A letter?"

"You've heard of it, right?"

"Ha-ha, okay," I said. It was actually a good idea.

"So, sis, tell me. Is Oliver a count? A billionaire?"

"He's seventh in line to the British throne," I said.

Amanda started laughing. Hysterically. We both laughed for a long time before saying we loved each other and hanging up.

Then I wrote the letter.

Dear Oliver,

I don't know why you're mad at me, but I want you to know I never meant to upset you in any way. Please let me know if I've done anything to offend you because I really liked our chats together and miss them. Not to mention the fondue. ☺

Your friend, Lucy

I sealed the envelope and left it on my bedside table to drop into the school's courier system later.

Soon there was a knock on my door. I'd been straightening up my room and turned to find Antony walking in with flowers.

"Hello there, Miss Tennis Star! Everyone's saying you're getting primed to cream Gagosian at the match next weekend!"

"Please. I'm a wreck. How are you?"

"Fine, just finished my flying lesson. You have to come up with me—it's so amazing, Lucy."

"I still can't believe they have flying lessons at this school! It's incredible."

He came up and put his arms around me and kissed me. "Even more incredible when you're up there in the clouds feeling so alive—it's a really sexy feeling."

Uh-huh. Climbing into a potential death trap at thirty thousand feet didn't really get my motor running, but I didn't want to wound the guy.

"What's this?" he said, picking up the envelope addressed to Oliver. I blushed nervously.

"Nothing, just wrote a quick note to Oliver—just about the match coming up."

"Oh well, I'm going to the courier office now on my way to the library so I'll send it for you."

"You will? Um, thanks, Antony—you'll save me the trip."

"My pleasure."

Antony kissed me on the forehead and left for his studies. I thought of what Rioko had said about Antony and Chérie, and about the day that I had seen them together, but if the suspicion were true, why would he be showing up in my room? I mean, it's not like I had any great magnetic force to keep bringing him back, right? Plus, I knew more than anyone how rampant rumors were at this school, so I decided to give him the benefit of the doubt and just let it go. Maybe he did shag her in the past, but this was now, and he was taking *me* to the Winter Ball.

Chapter Thirty-Eight

"Hurry up! You're gonna make us late!" snapped Antigone, who now insisted I call her Tiggy, which was a friendship promotion, of sorts. I had introduced the Diamonds formally to Rioko, who had until that point been invisible Casper style to them, save for the fiddle. But Tiggy, Iman, and Victoria took to Rioko's funny observational candor ("Moabi has short fingers like mozzarella sticks") and were happy to include her on our foray into Geneva to shop. The Winter Ball was only two weeks away, and we didn't have anything to wear.

Unluckily for me, the Saturday pilgrimage would probably not yield a thing. My body had never been in better shape, thanks to countless hours on the courts, but one thing not in good shape? My finances. I had spent almost the last of my stipend and was worried that the girls would be slappin' down the plastic while I opened my wallet and had moths fly out of it. Oh well. Maybe I could rent something.

When Tiggy's driver pulled over on the main shopping street in Geneva, Rue du Rhône, my eyes popped out of my head. Perfectly coiffed elegant women wandered by in five-inch heels, and uniformed schoolchildren hopped into chauffeur-driven cars.

"First stop: Valentino!" pronounced Antigone. "It's where I got my gown last year, and I am praying they have the right threads again."

The next few hours were a montage of feathers, sequins, silks, and velvets. Prada, Chanel, Carolina Herrera, Armani, Lanvin, Celine, Vuitton, Fendi—the works. I was practically dizzy. In each boutique, salespeople fell over one another to whisk us into a grand dressing room, serve us Perrier with lemon wedges, and show us the "perfect" gown for our ball. At one point, as Victoria was twirling in a purple chiffon frock, I heard two salesgirls whisper, "My favorite time of year—all those spoiled Van Pelt kids come cruising in for their ball with Daddy's credit cards!" They shared a squeal with dollar signs in their eyes just thinking of the commission they'd rack up.

And they did. Iman was torn between two gowns—one silver beaded gown at Prada and one luminous white one at J. Mendel—so she bought both.

Tiggy just loved a black velvet gown by Olivier Theyskens and snapped it up, along with not one, not two, but three pairs of matching high heels and evening bags for each. While Rioko was deciding between a Dior yellow one-shoulder, floor-length sweeping gown and an Oscar de la Renta pink confection, I decided to quickly run out and get some air. I'd spent the last five hours trying on gowns I knew I could never afford, and frankly the oohing and aahing over the other girls had taken its toll.

I don't think the girls realized that I couldn't afford the dresses, even though they'd seen the sad shape of my closet. I think they lived in such a bubble they had no idea other people weren't multimillionaires. I wasn't hiding it—I never pretended that I was in the market for a gown at one of the fancy stores—but I also didn't say outright, "I couldn't afford even a button at these places." I knew that it would just make them uncomfortable, and I didn't want to be in that sort of position myself.

I walked outside into the brisk twilight air and drank in the Geneva hills, the winding streets covered in charming cobblestones, dotted with perfect green trees, and glistening beneath the now electric blue sky. Around the corner, I saw a small gilded sign that read EMMELINE'S CLOSET.

It was a teeny-tiny shop—no bigger than my walk-in closet at Van Pelt, with a cool-looking thirtysomething woman reading a magazine at the counter. A little bell chimed as I opened the door.

"Bonjour!" she said as I surveyed the funky store, which had hot-pink carpet and leopard walls. "Welcome to the only vintage store in Geneva!"

"This is so cool!" I gushed, looking at the racks of old McQueen and Galliano. The prices were one tenth of what my friends were spending and when I spied a bin marked SOLDE (which meant "sale"), I suspected I might have hit the jackpot.

"All eighty percent off!" said the woman as I dug around in the bin, retrieving the most stunning crimson strapless, pleated Galliano dress. I looked at the price: one hundred Euros.

The saleswoman surveyed my find. "The button is broken so I give it to you for fifty!" she pronounced. I was floored. Fifty bucks? Okay, maybe a little more with the exchange rate, but jeez! Talk about a *steal!* That was the fastest money I'd ever parted with. She wrapped it with as much care as she would have if she'd sold me a five-thousand-euro dress.

When I reappeared in the Oscar store, the girls were stunned to see me with a bag.

"No way! You found a dress?" Iman squealed. "Lemme see!"

I was nervous about revealing the secondhand status but unzipped the garment bag anyway.

"*Chic.* I looove it!" Tiggy cried. "Galliano? So hot."

"It's so sexy yet classic," Rioko chimed in.

"It's very cool that you would do something different," said Iman.

"Well . . . " I was getting ready to tell them that I didn't have any money to spend on clothes, but before I could Victoria interrupted.

"*Love* it," Victoria gushed.

Maybe they knew I didn't have dough and didn't care. Or maybe they thought I wasn't that into clothes. It didn't matter. Either way I was just psyched to get a cool dress that everyone liked. We all left with garment bags over our shoulders, all the others spending more than a hundred times what I had. Amazing.

When we got back to school I was so pooped from our expedition I barely remembered dinner with Antony. He came by to scoop me up and I was flopped on my bed.

"You tired from your clothing orgy, my dear?" he said, sitting on my bed and stroking my hair.

"Oh, I got this great Galliano dress—"

"Nice!"

"It was at this cool vintage store, Emmeline's—"

"Ha! You kill me! *Vintage!* You're so funny. As if. " He patted my head and leaned in to kiss me.

His lips were soft, and while I usually felt a fluttering in my chest when we kissed, I was distracted, wondering why he thought that was so funny. Maybe people in Europe weren't as into vintage? Hmm.

Antony gently guided me back so that I was lying down. We continued kissing, and it started to get more intense. I hoped

Antony wasn't expecting anything. I mean, I was definitely not going to have sex with him. Not in the near future, anyway. Call me a prude, but I had seen too many girls on the base go too far only to regret it.

Antony gently started to slide his hand up my skirt and I immediately sat up as if the bed was on fire.

"What?" he whispered.

"Um, not ready for that yet," I said.

"Really?" he said.

"Yes, can we just keep with the kissing?"

He looked at me and I could swear for a second he was about to protest, get mad, storm away, but suddenly his face changed and he smiled.

"Of course, darling."

He leaned in and kissed me for another three seconds before pulling away.

"You seem tired from all of your shopping. I think I'll leave you be now," he said, standing up.

This was abrupt. "Um, okay," I said, kind of embarrassed. "Is it because . . . "

"No, no," he said quickly, tucking his shirt in. "I just think you should rest, and I need to study."

"What about dinner?"

"Oh, um, I'm not really hungry, are you?" he asked, pushing the hair out of his eyes.

Yes. Very. "No, not really."

"Great, then see you later," he said quickly, and was out of the door in two seconds flat.

I was stunned. What had just happened? I wished I had someone to talk to about it, but I knew Rioko was playing violin at the headmistress's cocktail party tonight and I really didn't want to reveal my prudishness to the Diamonds. I clicked on my computer and was forlorn to see there was nothing from Friend.

Are you out there, Friend?

I had really come to rely on this cyber person with whom I could be completely candid. I didn't expect an answer but a second later there was a response.

Yeah. How's it going?

Yay!

Where the heck have you been?

I waited and the response came.

Sorry. Wasn't feeling well. How's everything?

I couldn't type fast enough.

I just don't get boys. Am I naive? What is their deal? Sometimes they are so honest, other times they seem to play weird games.

It seemed like an eternity before Friend answered. I had called and ordered room service (chopped sirloin with Roquefort cheese and potatoes au gratin) and finished my math homework before Friend got back to me.

I think you have to make sure YOU are sure about the guys in your life. What do your instincts tell you?

Okay, thanks, Friend. I waited half an hour for you to be cryptic?

I don't know what my instincts tell me. That's why I'm asking you?

I waited and waited for a response. I was tired, so instead of waiting I quickly typed another response.

Have to go to bed. I hope you feel better soon.

I gulped down my food and got in my cozy bed. I lay back, worrying about the crack-of-dawn tennis practice, my strange interaction with Antony, and Friend's distance. Finally I decided to focus on the positive. I was definitely happy the term was winding down, and now, with my vintage gown, I felt that after tennis and final papers and exams I could finally enjoy the ball with my new sort-of friends and go out of the semester with a bang. Everything would go well, I told myself. I just hoped Sofia wouldn't be up to any of her old games.

Chapter Thirty-Nine

Oliver was friendlier at practice the next morning. He said hello, and when I rallied him, he even threw out a few "Nice shots." But he didn't acknowledge the letter I wrote him, and he was still kind of distant. I decided the only way to react was to be normal and hope that whatever was going on would work itself out.

After sweating like a pig, and enduring a grueling practice where Coach Sachs warned us every five seconds how we were lousy compared to the kids at Gagosian, we were released. My arms were sore from the massive amount of lobs and overheads I'd had to do. Coach thought they were my weakness, so he kept firing balls at me until my arm was about to snap off. I don't think he had any interest in my long-term physical well-being. As long as I played well for him, it was okay if in ten years I got arthritis or had to have all of my joints replaced.

I showered in the locker room, then started to head to class. As I turned down the path, I nestled into my coat. It was starting to get colder, and pretty soon practices would be moved indoors. It was high time. There had been snowflakes several days the week before and promises of big snowstorms this weekend. We had begged to at least do the playing inside, offering to run laps outside, but Coach Sachs thought that it made us tougher to practice in this frigid weather. I personally thought it was dangerous. Did he want us to be injured for the big game? I was arguing with him in my mind, not paying attention to anything else, when suddenly I realized that I was almost face-to-face with Sofia.

We both stopped and stared at each other. She was wearing all black, and even her face looked dark and sinister. I felt like I was in a horror movie and was the stupid one who said "I'll go check on Bobby" when everyone else knew that would mean I was the next to get the ax in my head.

"Hey, Sofia," I said. I felt my voice crack.

She glared at me. "You stupid girl. You are going to pay for what you did to me."

My stomach dropped. Like, to China.

"What do you mean?"

"You just have to watch your back. You're not all innocent as you pretend to be. I know it, but do your new best friends know it? Do they know the truth about you?"

Suddenly I straightened my posture. My mother had always told me to stand up straight, so I knew she would be thrilled that I was finally taking her advice. I hoped it made me look more confident. But it didn't squelch the fear that Sofia had set in me.

"If you say anything about *Gab!* it will only get you in trouble also," I said.

"Will it?" she asked, cocking her head to the side.

"Of course," I said with fake confidence.

She stared at me again. "Do you think they'll believe a scholarship student? You need the money more than me. Do your friends even know you're a scholarship student? What would they think?"

I was prepared for this. Of course I didn't want it broadcast, but I couldn't let that stop me from doing the right thing. That would be pathetic.

"Everyone I care about knows," I lied. Gulp. I hoped she would buy that.

"See, Lucy," she said, eyes glistening, "I'm smarter than you, I'm more sophisticated than you, and I have nothing to lose."

She quickly brushed past me and walked up the hill. I wished I had some comeback, wished there was something I could say to defend myself, but of course nothing came. To tell the truth, I *was* scared of her. And she was more sophisticated than me, at least in terms of doing evil deeds. Sorry, I'm not a criminal mastermind! I don't think that way.

A chilly breeze whipped across my face and then curled down my spine. What did Sofia have planned? Would it be soon? Or would I be skiing in France in twenty years and find her on the mountaintop waiting to push me over? How would I know? I just had to brace myself.

Chapter Forty

I was perusing the racks of leather-bound notebooks embossed with the Van Pelt crest at the school store when I heard Chérie's laughter coming from the register. She was always giggling excessively at whatever the male students said to her, so I usually blocked her out, but this time her hoots were particularly high-pitched so I turned to look. Antony and Rolf were standing next to her, both whispering in her ear.

Just as Antony leaned in to tell her something, his eyes met mine and his face changed.

"Lucy!" he said enthusiastically.

"Hey," I rasped. It was literally like there was a frog in my throat.

Antony came rushing over, as Rolf and Chérie eyed me curiously. "How are you, darling?" he said, pecking me on both cheeks European style.

"Fine."

"I was just coming to collect you. Can we go and have some hot chocolate?"

"Um, okay, but I need to pay for this."

"Allow me," said Antony, scooping up my notebooks and rushing over to the counter.

"Chérie, it's a charge," he said coldly. Chérie looked surprised at how frosty he was acting but marked it in her book.

"Come along," said Antony.

"Catch you later," said Rolf, who immediately resumed whispering to Chérie.

We walked to the caffè in silence. What was the deal with Antony and Chérie? It was like every corner I turned, there they were. I finally decided I had to say something.

"So what's going on, Antony?" I asked, hoping he would fill in the blanks.

"What do you mean?" he replied.

"I have seen you now several times with Chérie. Do you have, like, a thing for her?"

Antony gave an exaggerated laugh. "Are you serious?"

"Well, it's suspicious. . . . "

"Come on! I would never go for trash like that. Her father is a plumber! No, no, that's Rolf's bird. He just always needs me to cover for him because of Lena."

Lena was Rolf's Swedish girlfriend. Beautiful, but as cold as the glacier-filled country she'd been born in.

"But why do you have to cover for him?"

He stopped and put his hands on my shoulders. "Because he's my friend. Don't worry, Lucy, I would never cheat on you. And it really insults me that you would think I would go for a harlot like that. And she's from a pitiful family."

The last part struck me most of all. "Who cares about her family?" I asked.

Antony laughed as if I were a foolish child. "You're even more American than I am, Lucy. But come on, you know," he said, and commenced walking again.

I remained firmly in place. "No, not really."

Antony stopped and came back to me. He smiled at me, then kissed me on the forehead. "That's what I adore about you. You are such a good soul. You're not snobby at all."

"Why would I be?"

"You're right. No one should be."

"But why did you say that about her family?" I asked again.

"Oh, you know, her parents have three teeth between them. Her mother . . . " He looked at me and stopped. "They're just not the nicest people. You don't want to spend time with them. I'm sure your family is much nicer, but that's not even the point. I am wild about you!"

He grabbed my hand and I continued walking with him. We ran into a bunch of his friends and all ended up together at the caffè. But again I felt like there was some sort of disconnect between Antony and me. In the past, he'd made sense to me. But not so much anymore. Did I really know him?

Chapter Forty-One

*I*t was the night before my match and my heart was pounding. This would be my launchpad into the league's circuit because no one had ever seen me play and I had to either live up to the buzz or fade to anonymous toast. I lay there, thoughts tromping across one another in a confusing collage. What was up with my relationship with Antony? Would I bomb this game? What havoc would Sofia wreak on my life? Was it a mistake to come here?

As all these worries and more fiesta'd in my overactive brain, I slowly fell asleep. I woke up bleary-eyed and then focused on the clock. *Oh my god, nine thirty?!* I had arranged through the concierge for a wake-up call at eight! Holy crap. I was supposed to be warming up by now! I quickly dialed the front desk to ask what had happened to my call.

"*Je suis désolé*, I'm sorry, but zee record shows you phoned at one sixteen to cancel zee wake-up call. . . . "

At *1:16?* I was long in zzzz's land by then; how could . . . *Sofia!* That bitch. She was trying to sabotage me on my most important day at Van Pelt thus far. Evil. Serves me right for relying on such a fancy switchboard that the school offered, hotel style.

I bolted for the fastest shower in history and ran at top speed to the courts, which were a world away.

"Where you been, Lucy?" Coach Sachs demanded. I already saw my opponents—complete with their own water boys—warming up on the outside courts.

"I'm sorry, I . . . overslept."

"Overslept! Over*slept*? You think I ever heard Sharapova say that when I trained her? Get the hell out there."

I rallied with one of the assistant coaches for a while, and then Coach Sachs had us pack it up and head inside. On game days we had the whole tennis staff in full uniform with the Van Pelt crest in gold on the burgundy swish-swish zip-up suits. There were professional ball boys, refs, and ticket people brought in. I hadn't quite understood the need for the ticket systems, but then I heard it. The noise.

"What's that?" I asked. The subtle roar grew louder and louder as we made our way through the labyrinth of underground passages.

"What do you think?" asked Victoria.

Just as I was about to inquire further, we turned into the main door that led to the stadium floor. As the double doors opened in front of me, I was stunned to see and hear that roar burst into focus: it was the wild, unbridled applause of thousands. Not just the whole school, but also members of the community were there, freaking out.

I looked up at the stands, my eyes like saucers. It was huge! I felt like a total rock star. Though the match was an exhibition, it was really going to showcase who had the chops for the spring season and so, as Victoria had warned me, "Everything counts here."

I heard the announcer say my name over the loudspeaker and I could hardly believe it. In all my life, I'd never played at this level, complete with full stands. Coach Sachs sat beside me at my umbrella station and I caught a glimpse of the girl I'd be playing. In a word: *Uh-oh*. She was a six-foot Aryan Amazon type, with huge muscles and a blond ponytail that hung to her bum. She unzipped her Gagosian jacket and began practicing serves. Gulp.

I tried to stay focused and sipped some water as I looked up into the massive crowd. I didn't see anyone I knew! There was just a blank sea of faces. I scanned my teammates seated in the front row. The higher ranked players had to go first while the others waited. Suddenly I noticed a hand waving at me to snap me out of my outer-space realm. It was Oliver. He was smiling brightly and I lit up with happiness to have the ice now broken.

I took to the courts. I chose heads for the coin toss. Whoops, it was tails. They literally used an antique gold coin from Rome—apparently it was a school tradition. Amazon took her place and aced me. Right away, the first shot of the day. Darn.

The next one I valiantly returned, only to have her crush it back. The sharp "oohs" from the stadium stands were not helping; it seemed like my whole school was cringing at my screw-ups. She won the game. And the next, though by a smaller margin. After we'd hit 3–love, I looked back to where Oliver was, and he gave me a thumbs-up with an encouraging look that suddenly infused me with more support than the legions of cheering fans. Amazon, already complacent in her assured victory, was cockily waiting for my serve, and not in a ready position, so I caught her off guard when I smashed my serve with the fastest ace of the day. The crowd roared and the boom lifted my ego and serve higher. *Bam.* Crushed the next one, and the next. Over the next six games the rallies were killer and I had to fight for each point, but I'd proven my chops for sure. Yes, it took me a little longer to get in the game, but once I was there . . . I'd arrived. I'd picked up the first set, much to the shock and dismay of my opponent, and beat her 6–3. I headed into the second set on fire. And the flame didn't burn out. At one point, I faltered at 4–4, noticing Antony and Rolf laughing in the stands, wondering what they were talking about. But then I spied Rioko, Tiggy, and Iman, all clapping for me. Relieved to see pals, I crushed that ball into the last square centimeter of the serve box, acing her again, and ended up winning the match in an endless point that, when finished with a volley just over the net, sent the crowd to the moon.

I lifted my racket high, amazed that after such a stressful term of insecurity and outsider status, I could send the whole school cheering. I walked over to shake the hand of Amazon, who still seemed sideswiped by my late bloom in the match, and as I was turning away, Antony bear-hugged me from behind.

I was elated, but as we made our way off the court, I looked back at the stand where Oliver had been sitting. Empty. Angelina was there and gave me a thumbs-up sign. That was nice, but I had hoped Oliver would see my win before heading to prep for his match. Did he know how much he'd helped me? Would we get to reconnect and be friends again?

Chapter Forty-Two

When I rolled over the next morning I thought I would die. I felt sore everywhere. My arms, my legs, even my teeth hurt! After the tennis match, I had gone to the caffè in town and danced the night away to celebrate. I had thumped and bumped to crazy house music until three in the morning with Antony and Rioko and even the Diamonds. Everyone in the school was there partying, and I was a little bit of a celebrity since I had beaten a Gagosian.

But this morning I was in agony. The worst part was that it

was the night of the ball. Like, the most important social event of the year! And I was going to need a bottle of Advil to get me out of bed.

"Lucy, you awake?" Rioko shouted from the hall.

I opened my door to find her standing there in her robe, holding two jewelry boxes.

"Sorry if I wake you, but what do you think, red or blue necklace?"

She snapped open both cases and revealed the most gorgeous ruby necklace and an exquisite sapphire necklace that took my breath away.

"Wow, Rioko, those are drop-dead!" I said.

"I know, I know. But which one with the dress? I don't want to look like the cheesy romance novelist who wears gobs of jewelry."

"Why don't we wait and see when you are actually trying on the dress?"

"Good idea; I didn't even think of this," she said with a sigh of relief. "Hey, do you want to get ready together?"

"Sure," I said. "Let me just hop in the shower."

By the time I was done with the shower, the "team" had arrived and Rioko was already getting ready. The "team" was a personal hairdresser for each of us, a makeup artist, two manicurists, and a reflexologist to make sure any unwanted anxiety was rubbed away. When I'd tried to protest that I didn't need any help getting ready (because seriously, how could I afford it?), Rioko didn't want to hear it, and paid for it as a surprise. It was totally decadent, but this was a tradition at Van Pelt. They took these events *beyond* seriously. I mean, extra security was called in to guard jewels, and Europe's top chefs were flown in to make us an incredible meal. The band for the ball had played at Charles and Camilla's nuptials, and there was to be a special "surprise" entertainer who would bring down the house at the end of the night. Last year it was Jennifer Lopez. The year before? Elton John. Even the Rolling Stones had played when one of Mick's kids attended Van Pelt. Insanity.

"This is the life," I said as I leaned back on my bed and let the reflexologist massage my feet. I was in heaven.

The previous night I'd had a lot of fun with Antony. He was so thrilled that I won the match, and I think he was also proud that he was *with* me. All night people kept coming up to me and congratulating me, and every time he would put his arm around me, like I was his trophy. And it felt nice. Well, most of the time. There was one moment, when Oliver came over and gave me a peck in that polite British schoolboy way and told me I was "brilliant on the court," that I wished Antony was not hovering around. Oliver's eyes darted from me to him and it looked like he wanted to say something more, but then Antony burst into his rant of how awesome I was, his "little cutie," and then Oliver left quickly. I didn't see him for the rest of the night.

And now I was going to the ball with Antony. I was excited, but I still wished I were going with Oliver. I felt terrible about that. But the heart wants what it wants.

"Hello? Lucy?"

Rioko's voice woke me from my daydream. I sat up.

"Huh?"

A big smile flashed across her face. "Thinking about your man?"

"Yeah," I said. I almost wanted to tell her. To confide in her that I wasn't into Antony, that I wanted Oliver, when suddenly something caught my eye out the window. And that something was Oliver. He was walking across the lawn toward our dorm. My heart started beating faster. Had my prince come for me? I sounded like such a loser. But what if? Then, as quickly as my thoughts had appeared the bubble popped, and I saw Angelina walking toward Oliver. He smiled and gave her a peck on the cheek, and then handed her a small white rose corsage. They both laughed as if he had told a joke, and then parted. My heart sank to the bottom of the ocean. Like that heart thing the old lady chucked into the water in *Titanic*.

"Are you okay?" asked Rioko, noticing my grimace.

"Yeah," I said softly.

She looked at me curiously, and before I could explain there was a knock on the door.

"Who is it?" I yelled as the hairdresser tugged at my hair and the manicurist filed away.

"Delivery!" boomed the voice on the other side of the door.

"Maybe it's a corsage for you!" said Rioko with excitement.

Rioko was genuinely happy for me that I had a date. She knew that I had my concerns about Antony, as did she, but she was such a positive person that once I said he was okay, she had chosen to look favorably on him. She even said she was living vicariously through me because her date for the evening was the oboeist from her orchestra, a large German boy who unfortunately resembled Augustus Gloop from *Charlie and the Chocolate Factory*.

"Come in!" I yelled.

The door opened and a deliveryman with a large wrapped bouquet stood on the threshold.

"Delivery from Antony for Lucy Peterson," he announced.

I couldn't help but smile. So, Antony had come through and sent me flowers. That was so nice. Okay, maybe they weren't from Oliver, but hey, what girl will turn down a boy who sends her flowers?

"I'll sign for you," said Rioko, hopping up from her makeup chair. "This is so fantastic!"

For the first time I felt a flutter of excitement for the night's festivities. Rioko handed me the package, and I carefully started unwrapping the flowers.

"Come on, just rip it open!" said the hairdresser.

"No, she wants to savor it," said Rioko. "That's smart."

I felt like I was peeling the paper from a delicious ice-cream cone. I swirled the paper round and round until I finally reached the flowers and . . . gasped.

"What the bloody hell is that?" squealed the makeup artist, a chatty British woman who had just been on tour with Christina Aguilera and was full of gossip about her makeup habits.

The flowers looked like dead weeds. They were painted black and had that sickening stench of rotting plants.

"It must be a mistake," said Rioko.

"Let me look at the card," I said. It must be, I thought. Then I read the card:

I would never go to the ball with you, slut. Antony.

I thought I would throw up. I jumped up, handed Rioko the card, and threw the flowers in the bathroom garbage.

"This can't be right," said Rioko.

My eyes were stinging with tears. This was humiliating! Horrible!

"Why would he do this?" I asked, the tears starting to flow.

"Don't cry, love, I just did your makeup," said the makeup artist, attempting a joke.

Rioko came into the bathroom with me and closed the door.

"Did something happen last night?" she asked carefully.

"No, we had a great time. Everything was good."

I went through the entire night in my mind. We danced, he walked me back to the dorm. We made out, and that was that. Maybe he wanted to get more busy with me? Had I rebuffed him? But I thought we had an understanding. And why would he call me a slut?

"You have to call him," advised Rioko.

"Are you high? There's no way I'm calling him."

"Then let me."

She started to pick up the phone and I stopped her. "Please! Don't do that. It's humiliating."

"But we have to find out why."

"Okay," I said, relenting. "But you call and, like, pretend you want to find out what time he's picking me up. Pretend the flowers haven't gotten here yet."

"Okay," said Rioko.

She dialed his number on her cell phone and we waited as if we were contestants on *American Idol* trying to find out if America had voted for us. Finally Antony answered.

"Hey, Antony," said Rioko. She held the phone out so that we could both hear him. "It's Rioko."

"Who?" he asked—in my opinion, somewhat rudely.

"Rioko—you know, Lucy's friend?"

"Oh, right-o. Hi."

"I was wondering what time you're picking Lucy up?"

"Oh, we planned on seven."

We planned on seven! Rioko shot me a look. He didn't sound like he was about to bag.

"And are you planning on getting her flowers?" asked Rioko. I shook my head, not wanting her to proceed, but she shushed me.

"Of course. I'm bringing a lovely corsage. Don't you worry,

Rioko, it's all taken care of."

"So you didn't send her flowers today?" asked Rioko.

"No, should I have?" asked Antony quickly. "I didn't know that was the tradition. God, did I flub it all up? Shoot, do you know who I could call last minute?"

My eyes widened as I looked at Rioko. So they weren't from him! I signaled for Rioko to hang up.

Rioko quickly reassured Antony that he didn't have to get me additional flowers and got off the phone quickly.

"There's only one person who could have sent those," I said, arms folded.

"Who?"

"Sofia."

Chapter Forty-Three

So, after my graveyard-in-a-box debacle I exhaled and gave in to the wonder of Van Pelt pampering. I truly felt like Cinderella, minus the sweeping-fireplaces stuff. Sure, there were wicked stepsisters in my midst like Sofia, but they couldn't possibly bring me down. She had tried to foil me, but Rioko and I had won.

Or so I had thought.

After a delicious two hours of primping and plucking, my team pronounced me ready to go! I got up in my crest-emblazoned silk robe, hair and face glossed and powdered to perfection, and made my way to the closet to unsheathe my stunning vintage treasure. I unzipped the garment bag and found . . . tatters. Someone— take a wild guess who—had shredded my exquisite gown to fabric shards, with slices up and down the middle of the dress, making it look like fettuccine, like those car-wash slices that lather your wheels. I was beside myself—this was pure vandalism! I guessed I was Cinderella after all. And there would be no fairy godmother spouting "Bibbity bobbity boo" and making it all better with a flick of her wand. Defeated, I sat down on the floor in my robe and started to cry.

Rioko heard my torrent of tears and burst in the door looking ravishing. I was so happy to see her in total princess mode, I actually stopped sobbing long enough to compliment her.

"What happened?" she asked, looking at the tatters of my once stunning dress.

"I think Sofia the Grim Reaper took her scythe and sharpened it on my dress. Now I have nothing to wear."

The door, which had been ajar, now had three faces peering in: Tiggy's, Victoria's, and Iman's.

"That little bitch!" squealed Iman, beholding my rags. "You *must* borrow one of mine. I bought three different ones in the end so I could choose. You must wear one."

While I was deeply touched by the offer, I felt too weird taking a ten-grand gown on loan. What if I spilled punch? What if I tripped and ripped the skirt?

"You're so sweet, but . . . it's okay. I guess I can wear this short black one I have."

"Nonsense!" exclaimed Antigone. "Let me see this," she said, examining my snipped dress. "Okay. It does look as if Edward Scissorhands designed it, but may I remind you of Alexander McQueen's winter 2006 collection?"

We all stared at her blankly. I was relieved to see even Iman and Victoria didn't have that runway show on mental file.

"Helloo?" Antigone said, appalled, as if we had gaping holes in our fashion education or couture Alzheimer's. "Remember the cuts? He sliced them *on purpose* and then stitched them up again! So chic. I'll send for one of the seamstresses to resew these and they'll look soooo cool! Just like that cover of Italian *Vogue*!"

It might just be weird enough to work! I thought. Within minutes there were two women with thimbles and pincushions going to work on the dress. And thirty minutes later, as my friends put on their final lip glosses and perfume sprays, the women emerged with my dress, which looked even cooler than before. It had gone from classic chic to edgy glam and, I must say, that Alexander McQueen was on to something. I zipped it up, elated, and linked arms with the girls to stroll toward the large foyer where our dates would be waiting.

As we all walked in a line through the grand salon to the gilded hallway where the guys were waiting in their tails and white tie, I felt cheered by the girls around me. I finally had friends. It hadn't been easy, and it took a whole semester, but it was organic and real, unlike my friendship with Sofia. And they had done what friends do—they'd helped me in a jam. And as I saw Antony waiting across the salon, corsage in hand, I had the feeling it would be a spectacular night.

Suddenly there was a commotion outside. Intrigued, we made our way over to the entrance to find out what the to-do was about. There were four of the most handsome white horses I had ever seen leading a gorgeous carriage. Seated on the plush red velvet banquette were Angelina, in a magnificent white gown with a white fur collar, and Oliver. My eyes locked on his for a second, and he reddened. An odd look flashed across his face as I saw him look me up and down. Was he embarrassed that he was in this rather ostentatious carriage? Or was it something else? Before I could process, paparazzi pushed me out of the way. There was a storm of flashbulbs, during which time Antony grabbed my hand and led me down the stone pathway ahead of the carriages and into the grand portals inside the ballroom foyer. Here we go, I thought, as the door closed behind us.

Chapter Forty-Four

The tradition was to walk through a receiving line, where boys bowed and girls curtsied to the deans and headmistress of the school, as well as the visiting royal representative (that night it was Princess Victoria of Sweden). Every girl, myself included, had received a pressed pair of brand-new silk white gloves for just this moment. I glided along the receiving line, with Antony holding on to my arm, and felt as if I were in a fairy tale. Royalty! Ball! Hot guy! I just had to pray that my Cinderella story would have a happy ending.

"You look lovely," whispered Antony in my ear after we had shaken hands with some diplomat. I could feel his breath hot on my neck and it sent a shiver down my spine.

"Thank you. This is amazing."

After we blew through the line, Antony took my hand and led me to the escort table, where we picked up our seating assignments on gilded calligraphied cards.

"Table thirteen!" said Antony. "Uh-oh."

"Luckily I don't believe in curses," I said halfheartedly. Right?

"Let's go," said Antony.

We glided down the long hall, which was adorned with breathtaking floral arrangements. My mother, an avid gardener who sets up her little plot in whatever meager backyard we are assigned to, would surely have been in Utopia. There were giant branches of the most beautiful pink dogwood bursting out in every corner. Who gets dogwood in December?

When we got to the end of the hall, two footmen opened the double doors for us and we got our first glimpse of the ballroom. In a word: *unbelievable*. In many words: *breathtaking, exquisite, gorgeous, fantastic, spectacular.* I felt like I was in a winter wonderland in czarist Russia. All of the tables and chairs were sheathed in a gauzy white fabric, and in the center of every table was a clear vase bursting with plump white roses. There were candles flickering everywhere, including white ones in the large silver candelabras that adorned every table. Dripping from the ceiling were hundreds of twinkling white Christmas-tree lights wrapped around green pine branches, which gave the effect that each table was being blessed by shooting stars. I had never seen anything like it.

Antony continued leading me to my table and held my chair for me like a gentleman while I sat down. I was enraptured and barely noticed when Maxwell, Rolf, and their dates, Tiggy and Moabi, and finally Oliver and Angelina also sat down at our table. I glanced around, bummed that Rioko wasn't at my table, but we shared a smile across the ballroom. I was so impressed by everything that it was enough temporarily to take my mind off the fact that I would have to spend the entire evening with Oliver and Angelina, who no doubt would be gazing at each other lovingly.

When everyone had been seated, a team of waiters came and pulled the silver covers off our first course in unison. It was a white cone-shaped dish in which sat a white eggshell half encased by gold lamé. Inside was a large dollop of sour cream topped off by a generous portion of caviar. The waiters immediately set about doling out mini blini to accompany it, as well as garnishes like capers, chopped onion, and fluffy diced egg white. It was so dramatic. Only, I hated caviar.

"Hey, do you want mine?" I asked Antony.

His eyes widened. "You don't like caviar?"

"I think it's kind of gross. Too salty."

He laughed as he scooped my caviar onto his plate. "You probably OD'd when you were a child."

"I never had it when I was a child. I didn't try it until I got

223

here," I said, reaching for the bread basket and tearing off a piece of rosemary-flecked brioche.

"Come on," said Antony.

"We never had it on base, believe it or not."

"What base?" asked Antony.

"My father's in the army," I said. We'd never specifically talked about my family, but I didn't want it to be a secret. It's not like I'd hidden anything else about my financial situation from Antony, and I would never hide where I came from.

He looked confused and his brow furrowed. "What? He's in the army?"

"Yeah, you know, to protect and to serve . . . "

Tiggy, who had heard the tail end of our conversation, chimed in. "Did you hear that Prince Harry is thinking of giving up military service? They say Harry's girlfriend wants him around more," she continued, taking a big bite of caviar.

"Is that true, Oliver?" asked Rolf.

I could tell Tiggy had forgotten that Oliver was related to Harry because she immediately turned bright red.

"Um, that's what I read in *Gab!*, anyway. . . . " she said, embarrassed.

"That's what I read also. That bloke doesn't keep in touch with the family. Probably too busy with the girlfriend," said Oliver, winking at Tiggy. She smiled. That was what was so great about Oliver. So many people could have made a big stink that someone was gossiping about their family, but instead he tried to make

Tiggy feel better. It also reinforced the danger of going to a school like Van Pelt. You couldn't really gossip about anyone because everyone there was related to someone rich and famous. And then you had people like Sofia who were lurking about taking notes. I shivered just thinking of her. I had scanned the crowd for her but didn't see her anywhere.

"Are you cold?" asked Antony, rubbing my back.

"No, it's okay, there was just a breeze."

Antony continued to rub my back. "Well, I wouldn't want you to get a cold. Your father would never forgive me. And now that I know that he can use a gun, well, that changes everything. Not only is he a corporate raider, he's got a mean shot."

Corporate raider? More like corporal. Before I could ask Antony what the heck he was talking about Rolf yelled across the table.

"So what was up with the cheesy entrance, Oliver? I mean, a horse and buggy? You looked like a tourist in Central Park."

I expected Oliver to get angry, but instead he laughed. "God-awful, right?"

"Did you plan that?" asked Moabi.

"No way!" said Oliver quickly. "It's an unfortunate tradition with my family—you know, the past members who have attended Van Pelt. I begged and pleaded to be let off the hook, but my uncle, who's on the board, likes to see me squirm, so he insisted. . . ."

I stared at Angelina, anticipating that she would be upset that

Oliver was so dismissive of what I thought to be a romantic gesture, but she surprised me.

"Outdated and tacky. Like royals," she said with a sly smile.

"There, there," said Oliver jokingly.

"Ah, she tells it like it is," said Antony.

Oliver shot Antony a look of contempt. He was willing to laugh at himself with people he liked, but it was clear that Antony was not one of them. Antony turned to me.

"We should all just buy titles. Sell them to the highest bidder. Maybe your dad could become King of England," said Antony, looking at me and then shooting Oliver a harsh look.

"My dad? Yeah, right," I said with a fake laugh. Why was Antony bringing up my dad at the table? I was really not in the mood to illuminate my financial differences at the ball.

"Lucy's dad just got voted the second richest man in the EU. That's way above your family, Oliver," said Antony, sneering at Oliver.

"What are you talking about?" I said, confused.

"You don't have to be modest," said Antony smugly. "It's cool that your dad dominates the steel industry."

"My dad doesn't dominate the steel industry," I said. I could feel everyone at the table staring at me intently. I so didn't want to be having this conversation here.

"You can stop, Luce. It's okay to be wealthy. I mean, I know you like the perks. Luce tells me that she won't sleep on sheets that are under a thousand thread count," Antony added proudly, staring straight at Oliver. I watched Oliver look at him and then turn to me.

"Are you kidding? I was joking when I said that," I whispered.

"Right. Like you were joking about how poor the maid service is, and how you fly your own planes."

"Yes," I said, my face red and hot. "It's called sarcasm!"

"But isn't your dad Robert Peterson?" he asked accusatorily.

"Yes," I said.

"Robert Peterson the steel magnate?" he asked with vehemence. I felt like I was a witness being grilled by the prosecution.

"Uh . . . no. Corporal Robert Peterson of the U.S. Army," I said softly. "Wrong Google result, I think. You must be confused."

Antony's lips quivered. "What the hell?" he muttered.

"Does anyone want to dance?" asked Oliver loudly. "The music is lovely."

Before she could respond, Oliver had grabbed Angelina's hand and started to lead her to the dance floor. On his way, I saw him tap Moabi and Maxwell, who followed suit with their dates. Soon even Rolf and his date got up and Antony and I were left alone. Antony wasn't looking at me. He kept sipping his water furiously as if he had just been trapped in the desert for a year and was totally dehydrated. I didn't even know where to begin, I was so confused.

"You bloody liar," he muttered, still not looking at me.

"Excuse me? I'm a liar? What did I lie about?" I asked, dizzy with humiliation.

"You let me believe you were rich. . . . "

"What are you talking about?" I demanded. "I was joking when I said all that stuff about the food being bad and the service being poor. It was so obviously an exaggeration. Nothing is better than this place. I've never had it so good. That's why I just assumed that you were in on the joke."

"Still . . . ," he said.

"I don't know where you got the idea that I was rich."

"In the facebook. It says your father's name, that you live in Germany, and there's just a P.O. box listed. . . . "

"Yes, I do, and all that's true. But it's a military P.O."

"Why didn't you tell me you were poor? No doubt you're on scholarship?"

I felt like I had been slapped. "That's none of your business."

Antony shook his head and whistled through his teeth. "Just brilliant."

Suddenly my blood started to boil. "So it *matters* to you that I'm on scholarship? Were you just dating me because you thought I was rich? And I suppose you really are hooking up with Chérie?"

I could tell that Antony was debating what to say. He was quiet for a moment, then threw his head back and started to laugh. But it was more like a cackle. The evil cackle that the Wicked Witch has when she's about to do something horrible.

"I'm not that sort of person," said Antony, abruptly turning to face me.

"Yeah, right." I sat back in my chair, disgusted.

"Come on, let's go dance. I'll prove it to you," he said, standing up and offering me his hand.

"No thanks."

"Come on," he said forcefully. He yanked my hand and started to drag me out to the parquet dance floor. At that moment I had a decision to make. I could break away and leave, undoubtedly making a fuss that everyone would talk about for weeks, maybe even months, to come or I could just go along with it. It took all my strength, but I decided to do the latter. I certainly didn't want to dance with Antony after what I'd just learned about him, but I didn't want to create a scene. I was done with scenes.

I'd heard of dirty dancing, but I'd never heard of angry dancing, which is exactly what Antony and I were doing. He wouldn't look me in the eye. It was as if my face were so repulsive that it would kill him to make eye contact. Not that I particularly wanted to look at him, but it was awkward to dance with someone whose head was at such an angle that all you were looking at was a mole below the ear.

"I'm done," I said after a break in the first song.

"What are you talking about? We've only just begun."

I started to walk away, but he snapped me back toward him so forcefully that my body thudded into his. Tears immediately sprang into my eyes. What had I done to deserve this? Don't cry, don't cry, I pleaded with myself.

"May I?"

I turned around and saw Oliver standing next to us, Angelina behind him. "I'd like this dance, if you'd be so gracious as to dance with my lovely partner."

Not taking no for an answer, Oliver placed Angelina's hand in Antony's and scooped me away. Talk about knight in shining armor.

"Thanks," I mumbled, semihumiliated.

"I should be thanking you," he said briskly.

We danced along in silence. I was still burning with mortification and anger, so much so that it took me a few minutes to compose myself and realize that Oliver was an amazing dancer.

"I hope it's okay with Angelina that you're dancing with me," I said, suddenly realizing how ticked off I would be if the reverse had happened.

"Aw, don't worry. She's a trooper."

A trooper? That sounded . . . not very romantic.

"I appreciate it. I guess you were right about Antony," I said, swallowing my pride. "I just had a serious wake-up call. I should have listened to you when you tried to warn me—" I stopped, trying to prevent the tears from burning their way down my cheeks.

"Don't let him bother you. He's a wanker," Oliver said with a smile.

I wanted to say more but decided not to. A slow dance came on and I nestled my head on Oliver's shoulder and imagined what it would be like if I were his girlfriend. Things would be so great. I wouldn't have to stick around the next two hours pretending to be into Antony. The rest of this night was going to be torture.

Chapter Forty-Five

*B*ack at the table, the main course was being served. It was Poulet de Bresse with rich butter oozing out of the first cut, accompanied by a rich risotto. A series of servers paraded to the table with our plates covered with silver domes, which were all whipped off at the same exact moment, followed by each server taking out a white truffle and shaving it copiously onto our risotto in synchronized movements.

Too bad the seat remained empty next to me. Not that I cared, but I looked around the ballroom to see where Antony was. MIA.

Everyone marveled at the amazing food, but I felt hollow inside. It was like New Year's Eve, where you felt such extreme pressure to have fun, but alas, the stars were not aligned that way.

"Where's your man, Luce?" asked Maxwell with a sarcastic grin.

"Bugger off, Max," said Angelina, who slid into Antony's empty chair. "You really talk too much for your own good."

Everyone at the table started laughing, even Maxwell, but I could tell he was mortified. The fact that Angelina, the most sought-after girl at school, had given him a dressing-down was humiliating.

"Thanks," I whispered to Angelina.

"It was a long time coming. The guy's a weasel," she said with a smile.

We both dissolved into giggles. And that was when I decided to try to let go of all my worries about what had just happened with Antony and enjoy myself. At least I was among friends, so it would all be okay.

So I thought.

Right as I was about to savor the last bite of risotto with a huge piece of truffle perched atop the creamy Arborio rice, I felt something wet. On my neck.

"Whoops! Oh my God, so sorry! I'm so clumsy!"

The gasps of my tablemates mingled with Sofia's acid voice. I simply stared at my lap, now dripping with the red juice of the Van punch, an annual ball concoction served in silver terrines with sterling ladles. Some had whispered that the boys traditionally spiked it with some Spanish fly to get the girls tipsy, but whatever the mystery ingredients, they were now soaking through my dress.

"Oh my God!" Tiggy leaped up with her linen monogrammed napkin and began dabbing away at the red river. "You bitch!" snipped Tiggy.

"It's okay, Tig, I'm fine."

"Yeah, right!" said Sofia snidely. "Too bad your prince charming was out of here the second he realized you're here on scholarship!" she said loudly to the whole table. There was some surprised silence, but then something amazing happened. No one seemed to care.

"Sofia, back off this instant," ordered Oliver, standing up. "Get the hell away from her."

"I don't know why you are all friends with her. Don't you know that she's not who she says she is? This girl is a fraud!"

I could tell that people at tables around us were listening. Victoria walked up from the next table over. Sofia stood there, clad in a short, tight sequined dress, teetering in giant spiked heels, looking like this was the moment she had been waiting for.

"Shut up. You're just being nasty," said Oliver.

"Oh yeah? Well, what about this?" asked Sofia, pulling out a piece of paper from her clutch.

"What's that?" asked Tiggy.

"This is a letter from *Gab!* magazine confirming that one Lucy

Peterson sold them stories about several students at Van Pelt Academy. It's on the editor-in-chief's letterhead and confirms that Lucy gave them pictures of Victoria's bracelet, snapshots from Jazzmattazz, as well as information on Maxwell's affair with the wife of a bank head."

I was sick. The silence around the tables was deafening. The band was on a break, so the only noise was the din from chatter at tables farther away.

"Is this true, Lucy?" asked Tiggy.

I looked at her. Then my eyes went around the table. I watched as Oliver, Angelina, and everyone else waited for an answer.

"I did help Sofia take a picture of Victoria's bracelet. And I did tell Sofia that about Maxwell."

My friends were shocked. I saw them look at one another and their jaws drop.

"But I never took money for it. And I never worked for *Gab!* That part is a lie."

"Why did you do it?" asked Oliver quietly.

"I . . . I was just playing a joke on Victoria. She'd been so mean to me. It was a prank. I know it was wrong and I apologize from the bottom of my heart," I said, looking Victoria in the eye. Her face showed no response.

"As for the Maxwell tidbit, I did tell Sofia, but as a friend. I never thought she would put it in the magazine."

"Oh right," said Sofia sarcastically.

"It's true! I told you that as a friend!"

"What about the other stuff? How come the editor says he paid you?" asked Maxwell.

"I swear on everything in my life that I did not take one red cent for this. I helped Sofia with one prank, that's it. She is the one who is on the *Gab!* payroll. Her father works there—they pay for her education, her clothes, everything."

"That's such bollocks!" said Sofia.

"She reads the files in the admissions office, and she has a spy ring that takes pictures. . . . " I added.

"No one believes you," said Sofia, crossing her arms defiantly. The silence around the table seemed to confirm her statement. Desperate, I decided to bluff.

"I contacted your former school, Sofia. They can confirm everything. That you are just a low-level, low-rent girl who could never make it on your own so you have to take down everyone else."

Sofia went off on a rant. "You little liar! You stupid, stupid, foolish girl. . . . "

And then something funny happened. As she continued her rant, Sofia's real accent came out. Gone was the Queen's English—Eliza Doolittle was back! Everyone else noticed it before she did.

"What 'er ya lookin' at?" she said when she noticed everyone starting to laugh.

"Um, nice accent, Eliza," said Maxwell with a sneer.

Sofia looked stricken. I expected her to freak out, but instead she burst into tears. I couldn't tell if they were real or crocodile.

"You all hate me! I never did anything to you!"

"Are you sure that's true?" asked Angelina with an arched eyebrow. "Because I don't believe you."

"You're just a dumb inbred royal!" snapped Sofia, tears abating.

"And you're a fraud," said Angelina evenly.

"Sofia Glenn?"

We all turned around and found the dean standing behind us in his white tie and tails, arms crossed.

"I received a box tonight with several tapes of you conspiring to bug this school, including tips about where your hidden cameras would be this evening."

With students from other tables now gathering around us, he reached into the tiered candle and rose centerpiece and plucked out a small black rectangle no bigger than a quarter.

"The tips have all proven to be correct," he said. "You have planted recording devices and lied and schemed with a trashy tabloid to denigrate our esteemed institution and students. Security!"

Three armed guards emerged from the crowd, grabbed Sofia's hands, and led her out.

Before they took her through the front doors, she turned and glared at me with dagger eyes. I was too stunned by what had just happened to do anything but watch her go. I looked around at my tablemates. I could tell they didn't quite know what to make of me. No one spoke, so I decided to take the plunge.

"I am sorry, everyone. Sincerely. I apologize especially to you, Victoria."

Victoria stared at me evenly. This was a make-or-break moment. But then she smiled.

"I'll forgive you. It actually was kind of funny seeing the bracelet in there," she said with a smile.

"You got caught up with the wrong person," said Maxwell, much to my astonishment. I couldn't believe this benevolent sentiment, especially coming from him. "It can happen to anyone."

I was afraid to look at Oliver, but when I did he gave me a slight smile.

"That girl is as conniving as a fox," quipped Victoria. "But I guess someone outsmarted her."

Who could it have been?

Angelina, looking as poised and beautiful as ever in the candlelight, cleared her throat. "Oh, let's just say a *Friend* was looking out for you," she said with a wink.

I looked at her, bewildered. "You?" I asked softly, amazed.

"I found a weird wire in my room a few weeks ago," Angelina continued. "I had my family's own private detective look into it, and we found her prints everywhere. Then they did a thorough background check and found out she worked for *Gab!* and had fake names, a fake accent, fake everything!"

"Go, Ange!" said Victoria, who was now standing behind Tiggy. "That is so cool and Interpol of you!" The rest of the

Diamonds gathered around Angelina to congratulate her, and the crowd started to disperse. The mood seemed to be set by Victoria—everyone was ready and willing to forgive my gullibility for getting caught up with Sofia's shenanigans.

As I dried off the remainder of Van punch from my gown, everyone rose to hit the dance floor again.

"So, *friend* . . . ," Angelina said, smiling at me, "I'm so happy everything has turned around."

"So you were my friend all along?" I marveled aloud. "Angelina, I'm so grateful!"

She leaned in, grin widening as she took my hand. "Well, my dear, as your cyber friend and also now your real-life friend, there's one more thing I have been meaning to tell you."

"Uh-oh," I said jokingly. "I think I've had enough surprises for one night."

"Last one, I promise: Oliver is not my boyfriend. He's my cousin."

What?

"Are . . . you . . . kidding me?"

"Nope. We're really like brother and sister."

"But . . . I thought you two were together. . . ."

"We are together. Practically all the time. He's one of my closest friends. Our mothers are sisters and he's like the brother I never had! But he likes you. And he knew about Antony's cheating with Chérie. Antony did the same thing last year with our little second cousin from Scotland when she wouldn't sleep with him, and Oliver knew it."

"Oliver tried to warn me. . . . I can't believe I didn't see it. Antony's so awful!"

"Well, his days here are numbered," she said knowingly.

"How come?"

"Let's just say, friend to friend, that my private investigators put counterespionage devices in many places to see who was sending photos of me to the press. And let's say they just so happened to find many, many recordings of Antony and Chérie, which have been delivered to the dean's office tonight. I highly doubt the school would be happy with the student/employee affair. I doubt he'll be seeing us in Gstaad next semester."

Incredible.

Just then, as the band finished their song, a famous DJ flown in from Berlin took to the turntables and everyone hit the dance floor. Angelina took my hand. "Come on, let's go dance! Everyone's leaving tomorrow for vacation, so we may as well party all night!"

Our whole class was out there shimmying together. Rioko spun me around and I was laughing, feeling so freed from the cloak of worry that had been hanging over me these last few weeks. I couldn't believe everything that had happened that night—Sofia was out of the picture, Antony had revealed his true colors . . . and I wondered did I dare dream that I had a chance with Oliver after Angelina's revelation? I looked around for him but didn't see him. After a half hour of dancing, Moabi yelled,

"After paaaartay!!!" Everyone started hooting and cheering and ran to the cloakroom, where staff held out fur coats and beaded jackets. Outside, limousines were lined up to take everyone dancing.

I looked around, still not seeing Oliver anywhere.

"You coming?" yelled Tiggy through her limo window.

"Lucy! Get in!" said Victoria, tugging on her sable stole.

I wasn't sure what to do because there was only one person I wanted to see.

"Hey you!" I turned to find Angelina looking as glamorous as ever in her floor-length mink. "My cousin says he won't be at the club but that you'd know where to find him. . . . "

I smiled brightly.

"You guys go ahead!" I yelled back to the Diamonds. "I'll see you at the dorm later."

"Try tomorrow, honey!" said Iman. "Have fun!"

As the fleet of sleek cars pulled away to take my classmates to dance the night away, I stood still, the crisp moonlight twinkling over the majestic river. Yup, there was only one place I wanted to be. I made my way down the sloping hill.

Chapter Forty-Six

I wandered gingerly down the solitary footpath in my heels, reveling in the midnight air and the smell of wood-burning hearths. As I saw the flickering dim lights of Le Ciel, I got my first shiver of the evening—not because of the winter's heavy ice-laden frigidity, but because of the excited charge I got from knowing who awaited me inside.

Sure enough, as I peeked around the corner of the crowded tavern's inner room of golden wood paneling, I saw Oliver, fondue pot waiting.

"Well, hello," he said, smiling.

"Hello," I said, grinning back.

I wouldn't say there was any awkwardness between us, but now that we'd both kind of put out feelers via Angelina that we were into each other, there was some definite tension piercing our normal mellow interactions.

"So, I didn't know you had family at Van Pelt," I teased.

"You never asked," he replied coyly. "Have a seat." I slid into the banquette beside him and looked at him, heart pounding.

"Look, Oliver, I hope you don't think I'm a scumbag like Sofia. I knew the second we played the prank it was a bad idea. I regret it so much."

Oliver stopped me. "Look, we all make mistakes. You were honorable enough to own up to them and to get out of the situation. I have to own up to something also."

Gulp. "Okay, sure, what's up?"

"Lucy, I feel awful for what happened early last month when I was so weird and didn't talk to you. Antony had been taunting me, saying you thought very little of me, and I thought maybe it was true, since you were spending all that time with him, obviously dating him."

I was horrified. "Oh my gosh, Oliver! You must know that Antony was lying."

"I suspected perhaps he was inventing these things, but then I saw you with him all the time and thought maybe you did despise me."

"No way, it's . . . " I paused, blushing in the firelight.

"What?" he inquired, looking at me.

Okay . . . the plunge. "It's quite the opposite."

As if reading my mind and knowing I would need reassurance after divulging that I was *madly in love with him*, Oliver took my hand in his and put it against his chest, then pushed my hair back from my face with his other hand.

"Lucy Peterson, I know it's only one month we'll be away for these holidays, but I will miss you. Very. Much."

My pale pink blush had now fully blossomed into a dark peony hue and I gazed at this guy, gorgeous beyond fantasy, as he leaned toward me for the most passionate, all-enveloping kiss I'd ever shared.

Later that night, as we meandered hand in hand up the glittering snow-covered hill toward the dorms, after hours spent tucked away in our corner table, I marveled at how things had changed since I had first arrived at Van Pelt just a few months ago. This imposing campus now felt like home, and some of these wealthy, powerful, privileged guys and girls were now my friends   *real* friends, who trusted me and were willing to take a chance on me. I drew breath and exhaled, watching the misty air form in front of my face, amazed that despite subzero temperatures, I had never felt warmer.